Tiger Lily

Part One

AMÉLIE S. DUNCAN

First Edition, February 2015
Copyright © 2015 by Amélie S. Duncan
Print Edition

Website: www.AmelieSDuncan.com

Cover Design – Damonza
Interior Formatting – BB eBooks

DEDICATION

To Alan
I love you.

CHAPTER ONE

YOU COULD ALWAYS tell it was Friday when the inter-office cat dancing videos started to circulate around the offices of Arch Limited. The little balls of fur were our ceremonial icons, marking the end of our work week. I used to delete them without a second glance, but somehow I came to count on them. So, between eating a forkful of lettuce and typing on my computer on this particular Friday, I perked my ears for the sound notifying me of those dancing cats in my inbox. Halfway through the turkey salad I had picked up from the Korean Deli on East 44th, they finally arrived, dancing and frolicking across my screen. Inside, I squealed with glee. *Yes!*

Yet, on the heels of that thought came, *I cheer for cats. I need a life.*

My lack of a life, or in truth, lack of social options to fill my life with, would have to wait. I didn't have much time left before my weekly meeting with my boss, Chief Managing Editor, Gregor Worton. So I printed out the Request for Proposal (RFP) he had forwarded for today's discussion on brainstorming new business. As a small press, we weren't an automatic send for high-profile clients. Fortunately for us, Gregor was a gifted plotter and found creative ways to "slip in incentives to steal *cough* win clients.

The idea of our little publishing house pursuing these clients wasn't as futile as contacting them had once been. Not since Gregor started finding the best needle manuscripts in the literary haystack submissions. He managed to catapult our writers to the lips of the New York Times and USA Today top sellers' lists. In a way, Arch had become the phoenix of publishing houses, rising out of indie publishing mayhem. And for that reason, I understood why Gregor pushed for Arch to try for the "big fish." Still, when my hand grasped the paper printout from my tray and caught sight of the "fish" Gregor wanted, I grabbed a napkin to cover my mouth to keep in what I hadn't yet swallowed so I wouldn't choke.

Jonas Crane?

I read the first line of the RFP:

Jonas Crane of Crane Holdings, former Venture Capitalist and one of Forbes Magazine's 'Top Fifty Next-Gen' and 'Successful Under Forty' for the past six years, is seeking assistance in publishing his first book…

Jonas wasn't just a big fish; he was a whale. And even with our recent success, we were a string and bent pin bidding to hook him. Still, Gregor was a dreamer, like my father used to be. I needed his dreams. They gave me hope in my otherwise muted existence.

I placed my doubts aside and quickly typed Jonas's name on Google and jotted down a few key points on him to share in the meeting.

Once completed, I tried to stand up but fell back into my chair. I glanced down and frowned, my favorite gray wool skirt had caught in the wheel's tread of my desk chair. Again.

I hoped I didn't get chew marks on the fabric or I'd have no choice but to place the skirt along with the others in my graveyard of mangled office clothing. Crouching down, I pushed up the sleeves of my turtleneck and held the wheel in place. As I eased the cloth out of its jaws, I examined my skirt. A grease mark. My mind conjured a memory of my father scolding me, "Salomé's strive for perfection by presenting the best they can be." *Ever the vagabond, Tiger Lily.*

Covering my face, I took a deep breath and started to ease my sleeves down my arms, but stopped, I was too warm. Luckily, Gregor's fan in his office was always on. He didn't seem to mind when I angled the breeze my way during our meetings.

The heat inside the office gave a false sense of hot weather outside, though in actuality we were in the middle of January in New York City. The air outside was notably colder and we were in the midst of recovering from an unexpected snowstorm. But, as was customary for the city, all the streets were thoroughly salted and plowed. Nothing seemed to stop New York from moving, and that's what I needed to do. *Stop thinking and keep moving.*

I stood, successfully this time, and walked the three feet to my boss's office, careful not to knock over the "lucky" pile of books holding the door ajar. According to Gregor, everything was lucky and had to remain just as he placed them. Eyes down at the floor, I planned a path to the chair across from him, presently the only surface without books and papers. His desk had the most organized piles, though there were remnants of old coffee cups and take-out containers. I found it puzzling he never lost anything.

Gregor's ready excuse these days was "that's what divorce does to you." Lately he expressed concern his divorce had interfered with his Midas touch and needed the clutter to help ward off the bad vibes. I bought his story a year ago, but truthfully, he should let me or the cleaners tidy his office. Of course, the moment I allowed that thought to set in, I would've sworn one of his "lucky" piles of papers walked away on its own. *On second thought, I'll leave the cleaning to the professionals.*

"Come on in, Lily," Gregor said, calling me back from my thoughts. He smiled brightly upon my approach and I sat down and stared across at him.

Gregor's brown bobbed hair and tweed blazers had most believing he was a professor instead of head of the company, but he didn't care. In fact, in some ways, I think he thought of himself as a professor as well. He was not traditionally handsome, plagued by sharp facial features and bug eyes, though his were a lovely shade of green. Nonetheless, the women around the office didn't seem to notice his shortcomings. Instead, they often gossiped he had a "je ne sais quoi" they found sexually appealing. I didn't think of him in that way though. Gregor was just, well … Gregor. "Sorry I missed your Alfred Hitchcock marathon Saturday night," Gregor began. "I'm not sorry I missed out on the dissection you call discussion afterward."

I grinned. "I thought you liked that part."

"You having too much wine and getting loud and silly. That's the part I like." He chuckled.

I giggled. "You get just as silly and vocal as me."

He stared at me in that deadpan way for a few moments before joining in and laughing. Gregor had been more than a boss from day one, when I stumbled into his office a couple of years ago. He ignored my anthropology degree and empty resume, and still let me pitch myself to him for twenty minutes before sending me off to buy a client a gift.

I reached out to hand him the papers. "Here are the printouts you wanted. So what's on your to-do list today?" I poised with my pen.

His smile upgraded to a full toothy grin. "Jonas Crane. That's all I want you to focus on."

I tilted my head. "Don't you think Jonas is too high up the ladder for us?"

"'We are the music makers, we are the dreamers of

dreams,'" he said.

I groaned. "Willy Wonka? Gregor." I sucked in air. "Jonas hasn't granted any interviews in at least two years. Not even to the top papers. We can't reach him."

"Poet O'Shaughnessy, Lily, not Willy Wonka," Gregor said with a lift to his chin. "As for Jonas, tell me what 'in' you found."

The "in" was Gregor's buzzword for his method of finding a way to engage a potential client by accidentally on purpose bumping into them—a civilized form of stalking.

I pressed a finger to my cheek. "I read in the New York Post a while back, Jonas is separated from his wife and doesn't live here anymore."

"Old news," he interrupted me. "His wife, Dani, acquired the Dakota apartment on the Upper Westside and lives there with their son, Paul."

I shrugged. "Sorry."

"Don't fret. I've got a better idea."

I lifted my brows. "Oh? The fact that he's no longer in New York and we have a limited budget for travel isn't a concern?"

His lips twitched. "My sources say he's been staying at the Waldorf Astoria twice a month for the past three months." He awaited my adoration, which I gave to him in spades, along with a dose of pride.

I sat up straighter. "You're brilliant, Gregor, but is Jonas that regimented? I mean, he met the Dalai Lama, dined at the White House, and trekked in Kenya."

Gregor smirked, as we both mused over my showing off research skills to make up for a lack of stalk-worthy contributions.

"Jonas is not only regimented, but downright predictable lately." He smugly grinned.

I sighed. I hated when he dragged everything out for extra effect, and was relieved when he picked up his tablet, indicating he was ready to tell me.

"Jonas Crane will be sitting in Sir Harry's bar around nine tonight, drinking Scotch, when he will spontaneously meet a beautiful lady from Arch," he said.

My eyes widened as the realization set in that his gaze was fixed on me. "Me? Surely you don't mean me. Mia would be better suited."

Mia and Seth from marketing were his go-to persons for these fishing expeditions, as they had no qualms in getting the business by any means necessary. Not to mention the fact they both looked like models and were ambitious, an intoxicating combination for most people.

His mouth turned up in the corner. "Mia couldn't get a man like Crane. We've crossed paths, and I doubt he's changed that much."

I arched my brows. "Really? I doubt he'd even notice me."

"Oh ye of low self-esteem. If I looked like you, I'd be sitting in Sir Harry's, but I don't, so you're the one. You're better suited for this. Trust me."

We sat there staring at each other as silence grew between us. Gregor had done as much with past clients.

And his divorce, though a sore spot for him, had been a marriage from one of his client trysts. So he wasn't asking me to do anything he hadn't done himself.

His thoughts on my ability to attract the target were reassuring after the recent end of my engagement. Nonetheless, I doubted my five-seven height and curvy figure would get me past "hello" with a guy like Jonas Crane. And even if my appearance somehow landed me an opener, what was supposed to come after? I didn't say anything Gregor didn't already take into consideration when choosing me and from his apt gaze, my lacking confidence wasn't dissuading him.

I narrowed my brows. "I know nothing about sales. What if I mess things up for Arch?"

His lips curved up. "That's why you're perfect. Well, that and the fact that you're … beautiful."

My mouth dropped open and I laughed. "Oh how the compliments are flowing when you want something."

"Lily, I'm still your boss," Gregor said with a slight irritation in his tone.

"Yes. Sorry, Mr. Worton." I brought my hand up to cover my lips, swallowing my smile.

He turned his head hiding his grin. "As I was saying. You're pretty, but you still need to look the part. So, take the rest of the afternoon off. Get your bitchy roommate to help you, but for god sake, go alone."

I dropped my notepad. "Downgraded from beautiful already." I couldn't help but mutter, but the stern set to his jaw this time sobered me, though the twinkle in his eye shone. As for my roommate Natasha, a blonde stunner, she might easily derail the situation, especially if she caught a whiff of wealth.

I chewed my bottom lip and stared at Gregor, noting the wear around his eyes. He had put so much into this company's success. He only expected me to attempt to speak with Jonas Crane. If he refused, at least I tried, and thereby fulfilled my part on his quest for new business. "I'll do my best," I said.

Gregor exhaled. "I have no doubt you will, you always do. But," he paused, "this will be different. Jonas Crane is going to want to do more than just talk with you." His lips pressed together.

My lips parted. "How can you be so sure? He's twelve years older than me. Urbane. I doubt he would be interested in anything sexual with me…." I let the words die off as our eyes met.

A strange expression crossed his face. "Some temptations are impossible to resist," Gregor said. He cleared his throat, "I'm talking about Crane."

He displayed his Rolex. "You have seven hours. Just start with a drink and chat," he said. "He'll enjoy talking with you."

I smoothed down the front of my wool skirt and focused on the stack of books on his desk. After several moments, he finally spoke again, "If you do end up having sex with Jonas Crane…."

"I won't." I jutted out my chin and moved toward the door.

"You don't have to," Gregor said in an even tone. "Just relax and be yourself. You'll do fine."

I nodded and started walking again.

"If we land Jonas, you can take my job," he called out.

I turned back. "Will I need to create a mess of manuscripts in my cubicle?"

He winked at me. "Well, maybe not mine, but I can promise you a promotion."

I smiled at him and turned away. I didn't want Gregor's job, not that he would give the job to someone in my assistant position anyway. Arch Limited wasn't my dream. I hoped to one day return to cross-cultural studies and transform my mother's legacy, Perchance to Dream art week, into a professional program throughout the world. Thereby making it a true Salomé Love Legacy in more than a mere title change following their deaths. This dream was what my father would call a "Salomé dream," bigger than sense, but smaller than our will.

A promotion would bring a raise and more money I could add to funding and expanding the program this year. However, I didn't want to mention this to Gregor and instead said, "That would be great, Gregor. Thanks."

"Lily," Gregor began as his green eyes bore into mine, "you're my best gamble. You're smart, hardworking, and truly genuine. I'm happy having you here. You do a great service to our writers, staff, and me."

My cheeks warmed. "Thanks."

I made my way back to my desk in a daze. I didn't

normally go out to bars, let alone by myself. In fact, I hadn't been out in months. But now, I had the green-light to leave work early and shop for the night out. Yet, as I turned off my computer and disconnected my phone from the USB port, I couldn't even think of where to start. Sighing, I searched through my phone for my roommate Natasha's phone number, sending her a quick text. I was as sure as Gregor that she would know what to do.

Hi. Client tonight. Upscale. What should I wear?

After a minute, she texted back, *Get your hair and nails done, idiot. Where?*

I pursed my lips. *Idiot?* She couldn't pass up the op-portunity to insult me. I typed out the message, *I have no time for your stupid insults,* and stopped. If I told her that I was going to the Waldorf Astoria Hotel, she would want to go, but Gregor had instructed me to go alone. I smirked and added, *New Jersey*, then pressed send.

Although we lived together in a loft in Jersey City, Natasha was a New York City snob and would never entertain the idea of going out for an evening anywhere in New Jersey. This was most evident from the next message I received from her:

Why do you want to go out in Jersey? You're too short for flats. Wear the designer pumps, skirt, birthday shirt, or black dress. No more replies. I'm out with Ari. Nxx

I glared down at the phone and I sent another one anyway. *Don't throw stones, dimwit. You're no taller than me.*

I closed my phone and huffed. Ari was Natasha's lat-est investor. She had been hinting around he might move her out of our loft in Jersey City, but nothing was concrete as of yet. I couldn't say I'd miss her, but I worried about covering her half of the rent.

My phone displayed 2:30 p.m. I had to hurry if I was going to return to the city and "accidentally on purpose" run into Jonas Crane by nine. *And I was just complaining about the cats and no life*, I thought as I stuffed my phone and a stack of notes into my purse before grabbing my coat and leaving.

CHAPTER TWO

AFTER TWO HOURS at Blitz Spa and a short trip to the Herald Square Macy's for an impulse buy—a black, faux wrapped pullover—I stood on the sidewalk and eyed the lingerie shop across the square. Should I? I covered my mouth with my hand and laughed to myself. Me and Jonas Crane? Although Gregor had warned me, I highly doubted Jonas would want under my clothing, and I didn't have a boyfriend to show off lingerie to. Then again, I imagined Natasha's snickers if I told her I wore my frugal stock under the black cocktail dress she badgered me into buying a few months ago.

I waited at the light and when it changed, ran quickly across the street to the shop. After being led by a pushy, but friendly salesperson, I splurged on a black push-up bra, to encompass my full breasts. I added high-cut black lace panties to my order, to cover what my ex referred to as my "fat ass," though I had never thought it particularly stood out from the rest of my body. I had inherited my mother's hourglass figure, but I did my best to hide that at every turn.

My mind wondered back to Jonas Crane. I had seen some photos of him online. He was handsome, to say the least. However, as my father used to say, "Appearance isn't everything," then again anyone I showed interest in he had something negative to say about, as if no one was good enough for me.

Luckily, my mother and I weren't as close-minded. We believed in things more important than solely discourse, like love, and understanding, kindness, and strength. That's what I ultimately wanted, along with the fantasy of Prince Charming sweeping me away and caring for me. A husband to settle down with and raise a family. Definitely not modern, but my dream all the same.

I finished my shopping with a stop at a corner shop for a two-for-one pack of sheer black nylons. Even though Arch paid well, I still held on to some of my college budget frugality. After all, I still had dreams to fund.

I caught a glimpse of my hair in the checkout line and thought a visit to the salon might help. I pulled out my phone for an emergency call to Dee Angelo's on 40th Street. Dee liked me well enough to give me his personal cell phone number. Dee's salon was popular; not just because of the miracles he worked with hair, but also because he gives his clients so many compliments they leave feeling wonderful about themselves.

Dee was the first person I had met in New York, aside from my ex-fiancé Declan and his friends, and we had developed a friendship over the years. Though we didn't spend time with each other much outside of the salon, we did manage rare coffee breaks to catch up.

Consequently, I had become Dee's "little girl in the big bad city." He took sympathy upon me as I blundered around. I routinely poured out my struggles and woes in life after college with him.

Dee always said I was his top customer and to call him if I ever needed an emergency appointment. Therefore, for the first time ever, I decided to try to invoke my rights by placing a call to his personal cellphone. He answered on the second ring.

"Dee Angelo's."

"Dee, this is Lily. I need an emergency 'hair esteem' appointment today. Can you fit me in?"

"For you, anything! But only if you can come now, sweetheart. I have a good fifty minutes between clients, if I skip my break. I'll get Rachael to boot my next client. She's always late anyway, re-schedules at the last minute, and never tips."

I laughed and sped up my pace. Dee always called it like he saw it, and didn't care who heard him. "Thank you so much. I'm about six blocks, no, five blocks away. I'll be there in ten minutes."

"Alright hon, see you soon." He hung up.

I ran off toward his salon, weaving myself between the people at the crosswalks, and made it to the mauve and black awning in less than five minutes. I pushed through the glass door and walked inside. The seats were full, as I expected on a Friday, but Rachael, the desk receptionist, waved me up to the counter. "Dee said to head on back."

I gave her a small wave. "Thank you." I walked past the desk and into the salon area. The décor was modern in style, with built-in beauty stations of mahogany finishing, black leather, and leaded glass. My gaze fell on Dee standing by his station.

Standing next to Dee, he was about four or five inches taller, bringing his height to around six feet. His slender frame was often covered in the latest trends—today skinny denim jeans and a v-neck print shirt—though he often said he wasn't the one that followed the trends, he set them. His light green contacts and shoulder-length relaxed hair definitely stood out. And with his flawless honey brown skin, he was as exceptional as he defined himself to everyone.

"Hello-hello, pretty lady," Dee said and motioned for me to take the seat in his chair.

I sat down and grinned. "You and Gregor are so complimentary today. You'll both be to blame for my out of control ego."

"If only we could," Dee said. He shook his head. "I'd think you were fishing for compliments, but I know you better than that."

Dee was right in a way, but I wouldn't take either of their compliments to heart. I wasn't bad looking. I had a heart-shaped face and what most would call a "button nose," which I inherited from my mother as well as my long, black sleek hair and large deep-set silvery eyes. My lips, however, a little too wide and full, were from my father.

I sat down in the leather seat. "Thanks for taking me on short notice."

"Well, let me get this long ass hair of yours tamed," Dee said, removing my hair tie as he tut-tutted. "Why won't you let me cut this?"

I made eye contact with him in the mirror and glared. Dee had been cutting my hair bit by bit every time I visited, creeping it up to below my bra strap. He joked about Mia Farrow's cut in Rosemary's Baby a lot and I feared one day I would zone out and find all my hair on the floor. "Trim, Dee. I mean it. A trim."

"You could pull off a Mia Farrow," Dee said on cue. "But keep on hiding behind your hair. Men will still find you."

I pursed my lips. "What do you mean by that?"

"You frump around town, but men still see you. They still want you," Dee said.

I snorted. "A man that only wants me for a short skirt is a man not worth knowing."

Dee rolled his eyes back at me.

"Men are visual, darling. Vis-u-al. Since days of old," he said, "the girl with the best draped skin fur got the men to risk their lives to feed her. Give them something to attract and they will listen to your feminism." He chuckled at himself.

I focused on my hands and didn't say anything.

Teasing me about my clothing was Dee's way, and he didn't mean any harm. I had pretty much convinced him that it was to attract someone interested in my mind. But in truth, my body covering had started from my relationship with Declan, as to avoid being accused of trying to "pick-up" someone else, though he vocalized often his doubts in my ability to do as much. Declan occasionally added a bit of physical aggression for emphasis. However, that was the past, and I didn't want to explain it now, so I drew from my old arguments. "If all he wants is a visual, then all he wants is sex."

Dee lifted his shoulders, "So? What's wrong with sex?"

I blushed and avoided the question. *Nothing, when you're getting it.* "I came here for a boost, Dee."

He beamed. "When I'm through with you," he continued, "even you won't be able to doubt how gorgeous you are." He wasn't joking. He took my thick, straight hair and added large body wave curls. He threaded my eyebrows, and even did my make-up. Lifting the mirror when he finished, his face lit up and my heart squeezed.

"You're beautiful," he said.

I could only stare. It was my mother's face staring back at me.

What would she say if she could see me now?

My mind pulled up a flash of pictures drawn by her first grade class. They all featured her as a wing-clad angel, hovering over Marymount Elementary. *No time for that now.*

I threaded my fingers together and stared at my skirt. "Thank you so much, Dee."

He bent down and gave me a hug. I, in turn, ended up holding on to him longer than was polite, but I didn't care. I missed hugs and kisses. My parents used to kiss and hug me all day. Declan used this desire of mine for physical touch to his advantage most of our relationship. Often threatening to leave me at every turn if I didn't conform to whatever he wanted of me. But that didn't change a thing. I ended up alone anyway, missing the physical contact and connection. Truthfully, I'm starved for touch.

"There, there, Lily girl. You're good. I was only teasing you," Dee said as he eased himself out of my arms. He winked at me. "You are beautiful. Now go out there and bring him to his knees."

My cheeks warmed. "No dirty talk."

He chuckled. "I didn't go there, you did."

My cheeks heated up all the more. "Yeah. Thanks again, Dee."

I walked out of the salon and did one of my favorite things to do in the city, walk through the Time Square subway station. I needed the PATH train back to Jersey City anyway, but there was always something thrilling about going down to the underground subway to me. The sweltering heat and congestion, impromptu performances, and beautiful little children and families. There was always a new story to see there.

When I stepped off the escalator at the entrance, the

vibe was already abuzz with open guitar cases and the contorting limbs of artists scattered in my path. New York City. Nothing like it.

This eclectic mix of people was one of the first things I admired about the city when my best friend Mary and I visited during spring break of our sophomore year. That was also when I met Declan. I stared off as that first encounter replayed in my mind.

"Hey… give me your phone number, I wanna take you out anywhere you wanna go."

"I live in Boston, I'm on college break … I doubt you'll call or remember. You're drunk. My name's Lily, by the way…."

Declan hadn't even asked for my name. *Was he drunk?* Drinking wasn't his issue, at least not back then. He was true to his word, though. *But oh!* From that night on, Declan pursued me. He sent flowers, cards, and called every day because he "missed me," He kept saying he wanted to fly me up for a dream date that would include front row seats for *La Boehme* at the Lincoln Center, followed by a romantic dinner at the five star River Café. His strength and determination captivated me.

Declan, I sighed. I had been intrigued, seduced by his attention. He was my first love and lover. The one that stood up for me to my parents' and brought me out from under them in Quincy. My parents meant well, but I was their only child. They had me later in life and were at times overprotective, keeping me close in their circle at home. Sure I made friends, but not without getting their stamp of approval. Declan didn't follow their rules and didn't come up for a meeting before I flew down for our date. It was the first time ever in my life I went against my parents' wishes and returned to New York City to see him.

Declan had assured me, no expectations when I agreed and came down for our date. My lack of experience with dating, and all that goes along with it, didn't seem to bother him. He even offered me his spare room in his Chelsea apartment when I came to visit.

During our show and dinner, he was respectful, though he left no doubts that he wanted me sexually. What surprised me was that he acted on impulse, something I had never experienced before. Sure, I dated through high school and even college, and I had gonet as far as oral sex, but not intercourse. None of my partners had ever pushed beyond my boundaries. All respected and understood my desire to hold onto my virginity until marriage, something instilled in me in my upbringing. Something my mother did with my father and encouraged for me to do as well. And then there was Declan. He had no boundaries, just touched and caressed me. Admittedly, it thrilled me. So when we got back to his place that night and were making out, my conscience struggled as we grew closer to intercourse.

"I don't know you well enough. I don't do casual sex," I said to him.

"I don't think of you as casual sex," he said, stroking my thigh.

"I would only have sex if I am in a committed relationship. One that led to marriage."

"I want that, too. I know we just met, but, I want you to be my girlfriend. We can work it out. I swear. I would like a relationship with you. I can see a future with you."

That promise of a future was all it took, and I gave myself completely. My stomach lurched as bile rose in my throat. I hadn't thought about that in a long time. Now it seemed so false. Still, during those three years of our relationship, Declan was my champion; taking me into his world. Hell, he even drove to Boston back then to get me. He made me feel wanted, desired. Something even my parents couldn't challenge.

My mind returned to the subway, and as I walked on, the sound of someone playing a violin crossed my ears.

The performance of the day struck my senses and awakened me from my stupor and place along the white tiled wall. Someone was playing *Tchaikovsky's Violin Concerto*. My father held a great fondness for the piece and would often play it, though as a principal musician for the Boston Symphony, the viola was his passion.

I peered through the crowded underground in pursuit of the source. Would my father have considered this performance overdone? He could be quite critical, but he placed the same critique upon himself. He was always striving and pushing me to work harder to try to achieve it.

"Allegro vivacissimo," the music is almost over. I had reached the golden winged train mural, taking in the beautiful art and music right in the midst of the roar and rushing people at the Time Square terminal coven. I joined the small crowd gathered around the young Asian male in a printed T-shirt, so entranced in the music he played before us.

When he finished the piece, he immediately started to play "The Devil went Down to Georgia." The music brought up more sentiments within me now, of my mother and her love for the *Framingham's Joe Val Bluegrass Festival*. How she begged my snobbish father to play it for her, but he instead bought her a fiddle and taught her to play the song.

Boy, did he regret it. She played the hell out of that song.

My parents were opposites, but my father adored her. I had thought Declan adored me too, but he didn't. While my parents had often questioned whether he was good enough for me, in the end, it was Declan who decided I wasn't good enough for him. I fell head first into depression after their deaths and gained weight which was the deal breaker. He cushioned the blow by taking me to an upscale restaurant.

"Yes. It's not that I don't love you. I do. And you tried to be less spoiled, and I appreciate that, but you were thin when I met you. Aren't you embarrassed by how fat you are…?"

My stomach churned as I took a few dollars out of my handbag and dropped them into the musician's case. I next made my way downstairs to the 1, 2, 3 subway platform, where I needed to be to take the train down to Christopher Street and transfer to the PATH. My heart contracted as I queued and stepped onto the train, grasping tightly to the metal pole in the packed and cramped space by the sliding doors. No time for that now, I needed to prepare to go to the Waldorf Astoria and accidentally on purpose meet Jonas Crane.

CHAPTER THREE

M Y MAKE-UP AND hair survived with minimal damage after I got back to my place in Jersey City. However, I spent too much time in the city and found I had enough time to clean up and change into the black lingerie and lace flare skater dress I envisioned for the night.

Gregor approved the use of Arch's car service, so at least I didn't have to worry about getting there. Balancing on my four-inch stilettos, I settled down inside of the Lincoln Town Car moments before the driver sped off towards the Holland Tunnel back to Manhattan. I rubbed my hands together to warm myself against the chill as the winter's night had settled in and darkness had fallen over Jersey City. My apartment was only a short ride to the tunnel through the old brownstones, refurbished factories, and new high-rises. The traffic was mild along the two-lane roadway without much of a delay.

Before I knew it, we were across the Hudson River and heading uptown to 49th and Park. My eyes fogged over as we rode through the bustling streets. The sounds of the horns and music blaring were muted, as they had become so familiar to me now. In my own way, I had grown into a Manhattanite just as much as my room-mate. Still, when we arrived at the entrance of the massive stone and bronze illustrious landmark, The Astoria, my mouth dropped open. It was quite the sight.

My heart pounded in my ears as the doorman opened my door. I forced my rigid body through the entrance of the building. During my almost two years in New York, I had never been to this celebrated magnum opus of Art Deco, but here I stood in the infamous Park Avenue lobby. I tried not to gawk as I strolled past the intricate Greco-Roman mosaic sphere in the marble flooring. The ornate moldings, grand crystal chandeliers, and Doric-styled columns interwoven with heavy draperies and potted palms. This place was legendary for its opulence. Idyllically, I entered its universe of wealth.

While I hadn't gone hungry growing up, we were middle class, at best. After my parents died, I was swiftly relegated to living lower class. My choice of clothing, courtesy of my roommate, afforded me comfort in the affluent environment, and I managed to not stare in awe at the murals, and walk confidently inside the softly lit lounge of Sir Harry's.

The sleek mahogany bar with porcelain snack bowls dotted along the top took up a prominent portion of the room, and thereby was the first thing I noticed upon entry. Searching for a place to stand or sit, I zeroed in on one of the empty Japanned leather bar stools, and briskly made my way to secure the seat before someone else. With luck, I captured the vacant seat and swiveled around. Eyeing the eclectic mix of patrons, I stared over the high-fashioned starlets, middle-aged tailored gentlemen, and nouveau-riche designer clad tourists and wondered where I fit in.

Not sure, but I patted my back on arriving with ten minutes to spare before Jonas Crane was due to arrive. *Jonas!* It finally dawned on me I didn't have a plan for approaching him. Knitting my brows, I tilted my head down and tried to focus on making an impromptu plan. What would be a good opener? *Hello, yes. Jonas? Can I call you Jonas? I'm Lily Salomé from Arch Limited, and I'm your publishing house stalker, nice to meet you.*

Fidgeting and inward gazing didn't mix. At least not when holding my satin handbag with sweaty palms. Unfortunately, this realization came too late and my bag took flight, sliding across the floor.

Shit. I had barely made it inside the bar and hadn't even ordered my first drink or eaten a pistachio nut without embarrassing myself. Straightening my shoulders and ignoring the burning of my cheeks, I lifted my chin and eased over in the direction of my bag, doing my best to pretend I was bored and didn't care, or that I had maybe even purposely tossed it around. Spotting the bag, my insides winced at the polished leather shoes it had bounced against. I hastened my steps, but paused as a pair of large tanned hands with a golden ring on the left ring finger picked it up.

Gazing up further, I met the most luminous eyes I had ever seen. They were a rare combination of blue and turquoise like a tropical sea. He had black wavy hair that hung a little longer on the top and sides. Some lines around his eyes, but boasted of an otherwise flawless face. With a smooth angular jawline, straight nose, and well-defined cheekbones most women would die for, he was divine. Not to mention, full sensual lips were flashing a perfect set of teeth.

My hand trembled a little as I took my handbag from him, and recognition finally set in. He was not only gorgeous, but he was the man I had come here for, Jonas Crane. Serendipitous or cliché, it didn't matter. My "accidental on purpose" encounter with him had taken place.

The photos I had seen online didn't do him justice. Jonas was not only stunning, but magnetic. All eyes in the room gravitated towards him. Who would blame us? He was perfection, from his dark stylish locks to his impeccable suit that fit his frame like it was tailor made for him. His deep blue shirt was pressed and unbuttoned at the collar, exposing a hint of skin, and the thought crossed my mind if his skin would feel as smooth as it looked.

I would guess his height well over six feet, though truly he stood out and above all around him. Perhaps it was the way his presence commanded attention. What-ever, the case prompted me to inadvertently hold out my clammy palm for him to shake, which he took without hesitation.

He held on to my hand as his gaze roamed over me in a slow, deliberate manner. My pulse sped up as I followed its path from head to toe, with a lingering at the embroidery along the top half, the bodice of my dress, that had me shift on my feet. When his eyes met mine again, it was dark and penetrating.

My cheeks were already hot from embarrassment, but that didn't stop me from ogling him, though I tried my best to stop. "Thank you. Thanks a lot."

"You're welcome, I'm Jonas Crane," he said, the corner of the right side of his lip raised. My brows rose and my lips parted in an 'O.'

Jonas squinted. "But I believe you know that." He had a velvety richness to the tone of his voice that left me wanting to hear more.

I moved to take my hand back, but he held on, awaiting a response from me.

My breath hitched, "I do. Yes. I'm ... I'm Lily Salomé. Just Lily, Mr. Crane." I stammered.

"Jonas, please, Lily. I saw you walk in." He let go of my hand and chuckled as I wiped my clammy hand on my dress.

My face burned. He saw my grand entrance! "Sorry," I said softly. His stare was fixed, concentrated on me as if waiting for me to say more, but I had found myself stumped in front of him, only heightening my awkwardness.

Avoiding direct eye contact, I stopped gaping at him

and reigned myself in, by stilling my trembling hands that were poised to release my handbag again. My thoughts not releasing me from my clumsy entrance, gawking, and clammy handshake. I managed to blow my opportunity in less than ten minutes! I started to edge away, but to my surprise, Jonas took my elbow and steered me to his side.

"Would you like to share a drink with me, Lily?" Jonas asked, but his act of positioning me at his side answered his question. Truthfully, I didn't mind, though I found it surprising.

I glanced over at him, and fidgeted. Not knowing how to act or be. Especially when I found his attention steady on me. It was like being under a magnifying glass. Every part of my body lit and tempted by him.

"Do I make you nervous?" Jonas asked another question, and this time I answered.

"Yes, you do actually." My blunt answer earned me another flash of his gorgeous smile and gave me the impression he was aware of the affect he had on me. As striking as he was, it was likely a common occurrence.

"So what can I do to make you less nervous?" Jonas stepped close and I fought to get my pulse under control.

Not that. I shrugged and grinned. "I have no idea."

His gaze dropped to my lips, and I found myself leaning a little closer to him. What was I doing?

Jonas grinned and motioned for the bartender to come over, simultaneously asking, "What would you like to drink?"

Shifting on my feet, I worked to bring my mind back to task. I came here for my job to meet him and even though I recognized him, a drink could still be my "in" to discuss Arch, which put me right on plan. "Sure. Okay. Um … Merlot." The only drink that came to mind in the moment.

Jonas turned and placed the order, including a Scotch neat for himself, just as Gregor had predicted. He was kind of scary in his stalking, but nevertheless, I was impressed.

"Are you a guest at the hotel?" Jonas asked, pulling me from my thoughts.

"I'm not?" It came out as a question. I didn't have a good script in mind as everything was happening so fast. "No. I'm not. Just here for a drink." I fidgeted.

His sea blue eyes went stormy and he tapped his hand on the bar. "I suspect there's more. So you might as well tell me."

I took in a short breath. The way he said it came out as a command and I found myself answering without thinking. "You're right. I had rehearsed an introduction, before my handbag sailed across the room and hit your shoes. Anyway, I work for Arch Limited Publishing House and…."

"And you came to discuss my book," Jonas finished for me. His lips pressed together.

I eyed him sheepishly. "You don't have to buy me a drink or anything. It was rude."

My eyes focused on the opening along the collar his

shirt. "I apologize. This isn't … I'm sorry."

Jonas held the glass of wine out, brushing his fingers with mine and sending an electric jolt through me. I never had this reaction to anyone before, and didn't know what to make of it. *Liquid courage.* I tipped my glass back for a generous sip.

He chuckled. "It's fine. But I'd prefer not to talk business."

I nodded. "I understand." I understood he didn't want to talk about his book, but why offer a drink to me when he was now aware I came to do as much? I glanced up at him and found his gaze was steady on me, which sent a fluttering through my stomach.

"So, you're an editor at Arch?" Jonas asked.

I shook my head. *He's asking me about work. Perhaps business isn't completely off limits.* "Not exactly. I work more as a publishing assistant for the chief managing editor, Gregor Worton."

His eyes flashed and he gave a curt nod, but his gaze hadn't left me nor did he speak, so I continued.

"I do some preliminary reviews of manuscripts and editing here and there … I was an Anthropology major in college."

He tilted his head, and his lips curved. "Socio-cultural, biological, linguistic?"

My jaw dropped. *He understands Anthropology?* "Cultural studies. My passion lies in cross-cultural research and studies. I'm most interested in the research related to creating new dialogue and voices in cultural exchange." I jabbered. *I'm boring him to death.* I flushed. But when I peeked at him, I found his focus hadn't detoured. In fact, he was grinning at me.

I licked my lips. "Sorry. I can ramble on; I rarely get to speak about cross-cultural studies. I didn't mean to go off on a tangent."

Jonas took a sip of his scotch. "No need to apologize. I find it ... refreshing." He cleared his throat, "Where did you attend college?"

I put my glass down and pushed my hair over my shoulders. His gaze followed and I tried to will away the butterflies in my belly. "Boston University. I'm from Massachusetts, actually Quincy. I grew up in Quincy."

Jonas kept a grin on his face as he listened. I could only imagine him thinking Arch were silly in sending me. *Who are you?* I thought angrily to myself. I wasn't this bad at conversing, but with Jonas I didn't seem to be able to keep myself together. He unhinged me.

He touched my arm lightly and a tremor went through me as the electrical current flared between us. Did he feel it? I allowed my eyes to linger on his that were fixed on me and shuddered. He must.

Sipping my close to empty glass of wine, I gave him a small smile. "Thanks," I said quietly. "I'm nervous. I don't usually do the social side of work or hang out in bars to chat."

"You're doing great." He took a sip of his Scotch. "But how about you try asking me questions. That might relax you a bit. How does that sound?"

My face heated, as I noted the amusement in his tone and his closeness to me. *He's doing this on purpose!* I thought, grasping on to the little annoyance at him that crept in as I worked to unscramble my brain and calm my heart from trying to escape my chest. "So what do you do in your spare time?" Why did I ask that? It sounds like a stupid interview.

Jonas fingered the rim of his glass. "I have many interests," he said equivocally.

I rolled my eyes. I didn't think it wasn't going to be that easy, but I hoped he would have shared or at least said something. "Fine, I'll go first," I said. "I'm a Leo. I practice Tantric sex, and I sing to my cereal. What about you?" I joked.

Jonas stared at me as if I had sprouted a new head before finally laughing. I let out a breath I wasn't aware I was holding and joined him. A tingle went through me. He somehow appeared even more gorgeous when he laughed.

"You didn't like my answer," he said, his eyes glimmering.

I emptied my glass of wine and placed the glass down, "No. I understand perfectly. You don't want to share with the stalker that's hanging out at a bar trying to pursue you while you unwind."

"You're pursuing me?" he asked coyly, giving me a look that weakened my knees.

My hands shook as I attempted to place my wine glass on the counter. He reached out and placed it down for me. "I … I don't know."

"You don't have to answer that." He reached out and tucked a curl behind my ear. "I was merely teasing you, like you were teasing me."

His tone was soothing, though the sensation of his touch sent a jolt through my body. I took in a ragged breath. "I … thanks, Jonas."

"You're welcome, Lily," he said with a hint of amusement in his tone. He took another sip of Scotch. "Now to answer your question. I enjoy sketching, classical music, literature, old movies, Tantric sex…."

Jonas paused and waited for my blush, which I gave to him on cue. He responded with his own broad grin. "I also enjoy philosophy. Philosophy is at once the most sublime—"

"And the most trivial of human pursuits. William James." I met his eyes full on.

"However, philosophy is our inspiration, our doubts, challenges, what perception exists that does not have philosophy as its origin?" I said.

"Lily, now that's a dialogue we could share for eternity." His words thickened the air between us. The moment was palpable and I fell into it. His eyes blazed over me this time and a shiver coursed through my body. My own eyes were unable to move away from his, as my chest heaved. We were locked together, the distance between us gone.

It was Jonas that ended the connection by shifting his stance and running a hand through his hair. The light caught the ring on his hand, dispelling the connection. Was he still married? The rumor was that he was divorced. But with that ring still on his finger, he apparently hadn't moved on. Not that I was able to do anything about it. We both drank our drinks in silence as a distance settled between us again. I didn't understand what I might have done, but wanted to change it back. I attempted lighter conversation. "So, I hear you're in Texas?"

"Yes, temporarily. Though it's been six months. I try to return to New York as often as possible to be with my family." He averted his eyes, but this time I waited until I caught them before I started speaking again.

"That's good for you and your family. I used to travel often, but not much anymore."

Jonas motioned to the bartender to refill my drink, "Where have you traveled?"

My eyes dilated. "I went with my parents to Sweden, France, Scotland, Finland, and Ireland, all when I was nineteen. I also studied in France and Germany when I was in college."

"They still in Quincy?" he asked politely.

My eyes darted as I struggled to school my face. I was losing my composure in front of the man I was there to impress. *Not now*, I told myself. *He merely asked a simple question.* Where are they? "No. They … they're not."

"Did I say something wrong?" Jonas asked. His voice deep, soothing.

A lump formed in my throat, robbing me of speech.

He touched my arm and the flare of connection was there as before, but also warmth radiating from his hand had me wishing he would keep it there. My need for contact almost overwhelmed me in that moment. I tried to reign in the desire as I answered hoarsely, "Not at all, it was just a passing thought."

"It seemed like more," his tone softened, "or you wouldn't look so sad now." He reached out his hand and lifted my chin. I gazed up into his eyes as my pulse sped up once again.

"They're both gone," I said and sucked in my breath. He moved his hand down the side of my face in a caress.

"Saying sorry, isn't enough really," Jonas said quietly. "But I am."

I turned my head. "I'm sorry, Mr. Crane. I didn't come here to talk about myself and my family."

"Jonas," He corrected me. "And don't apologize. Truth is, you are my first genuine conversation in a while, besides my family…."

I nodded quickly. "Your wife and son. That's…."

"My ex-wife, Danielle, Dani and my son Paul. I guess I will be saying wife until she gets remarried, though," he said with a lift in his tone. But the cloudiness in his eyes led me to believe I wasn't alone in my pain. I reached out and took his hand and he squeezed it, then let go.

"Sorry isn't enough. But I am." I repeated his words back to him. Our eyes locked on each other, as we stood there, neither one of us saying anything.

"How about a change of subject?" I asked. "Could you tell me about your sketching?"

Jonas smiled again and I smiled back in turn as it was infectious. "When I have time I sketch people. I studied briefly in college so I'm not an artist as such."

"I'm sure your sketches are amazing," I said lifting my chin. "In fact, I bet a few galleries around here would be happy to have a few Crane originals in there."

"Sweet," he said softly. "To be honest, I do have a few sketches out there, but under a pseudonym." He took a sip of his scotch and shook his head. "Not many know that either. You seem to have a way of getting me to talk."

I ran my tongue over my bottom lip. "I was only making conversation. I didn't mean to pry."

Jonas leaned in close, and my heart skipped a beat. "I know and that makes you dangerous."

My brows rose. "Dangerous?"

"Dangerous and beaut—"

"Lily!"

My head snapped back as the sound of my name broke our spell. I found a man standing in front of us and realized it was Declan.

What the hell was he doing here?

I then remembered how Declan enjoyed the wine and dining at the "best of" in New York on the week-ends. From the Gramercy Grill to the Peacock Alley, which was in this hotel. My brows lifted as my gaze went over his grey suit, something he never wore, not even to my parents' funeral.

Built like a Rugby player, Declan Gilroy was six-one, broad shoulders, with a large chest, arms, and legs. He had thinning, ginger frizzy hair that he combed over, giving it a wispy, feathering appearance. His angular face was covered with premature wrinkles that made him appear older than his twenty-nine years, with a crooked nose and bow lips.

"Yes?" My voice came out rough. Jonas eyed him, but didn't remove his hand from my arm.

"Lily, what are you doing here?" His lips were curled as he took a peek at Jonas, who had moved closer, to the point of practically embracing me.

My lips turned up. *Territorial?* The possibility of Jonas Crane being possessive of me set off pheromones, though my attention was now divided between him and my ex before me. "What do you want, Dec?"

"Need to speak with you." His tone was sharp, but he surprisingly didn't try to remove me from Jonas.

"Lily. Do you want to speak with him?" Jonas asked.

I shook my head, as if to say no, but instead said, "I'll be back." Jonas let his fingers trail down my arm, creating a trail of goose bumps in their wake as he met Declan's glare.

"Okay. We'll finish our conversation when you return." He stressed "our" and that made me smile, despite the odd situation unfolding around me. I walked a few steps away and waited for Declan, who bared his teeth at Jonas before following me.

As we moved away, Declan announced, "This is my fiancée."

"You're engaged." Jonas raised a brow.

I jerked away from Declan. "That's EX-fiancée," I said, my voice slightly elevated.

I didn't get a chance to see Jonas's face to confirm he registered my reply.

Why it was important to me, I didn't know. None-theless, I had Declan now before me after six months of silence. "What do you want, Dec?"

His green eyes flashed at me. "Why are you being rude? I thought you Salomé's were never rude," Declan said with snark. "They strive for perfection, in all things."

My face fell. Declan had a way of unraveling me. He often mimicked my father on his Salomé third person speak. "I wasn't being rude. I just don't know what you want to discuss with me."

"I didn't expect to see you out. You look different," he said.

I shrugged, but inside I danced. Nothing more satis-fying than to look better than the last time you saw your ex. *Thank you Dee and Natasha.* "Yeah. I'd say the same about you," I said politely.

Declan smiled and moved closer to me. "I'm sur-prised you never called me. You don't have any friends here." He brushed his hands on my jaw line and down the side of my neck, which had, in the past, triggered a need for more. "You must be lonely."

I bristled and stepped back. "True. I moved here for you."

His smile wilted at the edges. "You couldn't find a job with that useless degree and I had to delay our wedding. You became—"

I gritted my teeth, "The fat spoiled princess."

Declan covered his mouth, to suppress a chuckle I suspected. "I said that in anger," he said once he composed himself. I stood stoic as his eyes assessed me from head to foot. "You lost some."

I folded my arms around my waist, touching my almost flat stomach. *Some?* "I'm done with this conversation."

I started walking away when he gripped my arm tightly. Any more pressure would leave a mark. I stared at his hand like I had so many times in the past, until he dropped it away. I flushed as I glanced around checking if anyone had witnessed it, only to find Jonas's face set in stone. I shook my head and managed a weak smile towards him. He didn't smile back, nor remove his focus from me.

"I was only teasing," Declan said, getting my focus back to him. "You know me, come on. But hey, look at you now? You look *cute*. I mean, what I want to say is, I miss you."

I paused as I didn't see any twinkles in his eyes or grin on his face. Did he mean it?

"Are you sleeping through the night now?" His tone was warm, as he made his inquiry.

I glanced up at him and smiled. He remembered, I thought as my mind highlighted the positives, as it often did between us. "I've been keeping busy at work, and it tires me out. I haven't stayed up all night in a long time now."

"You can always call and I'll talk you through whatever you need." He touched my arm. "Come over, make you feel good. You're still my good girl."

I didn't meet his eyes because I feared what he would find there. He experienced that part of me too often, and used it too well.

"Declan."

We turned and a tall and thin mousy woman with large brown eyes and severely cut bobbed hair approached us. She was wearing an ill-fitted gray silk dress.

"I told you to wait over there." Declan stumbled on his words.

She ignored him, directing her glare towards me. "I'm Heather, Declan's fiancée. You are?" Heather reached out for me to shake her jewel-encrusted hand. The iceberg on her ring finger almost blinded me and my triviality noted it was larger than the one he had purchased for me.

I blinked rapidly. I wasn't sure if it was from the ring or the crushing blow enfolding before me. "Congratulations," I said. She cleared her throat and turned towards Declan.

"We're not engaged," Declan hissed. He turned on Heather. "I didn't buy that for you to go around—"

"Just leave me alone, Dec." I bit the inside of my cheek as I walked away.

"I'll call you, Lily," Declan said, before turning his wrath on Heather.

"Please don't." I stumbled away and headed towards the bar exit for home. As I reached the door, I felt a hand at my elbow. I was tempted to pull away, but I turned and found Jonas, his face set in a concerned expression.

"Lily, what happened?" Jonas asked.

Tears rose within me and filled my eyes. Without a word, he reached out and pressed his hand on the small of my back and led me out of the bar and into the lobby of the hotel.

When we stopped, I stared down at my heels. "I'm sorry, Jonas. I'm not up for more conversation tonight." I choked. He lifted my chin up to meet his eyes, and I trembled.

"I'm not leaving you alone crying," he said.

I turned my head. "I'm not crying. I'm just … shocked. He's engaged." I covered my mouth with my hands. He stepped close. So close I could feel the heat of his body behind me. I inhaled and took in his scent, some type of expensive cologne or aftershave. My body hummed. *If I stepped back would he engulf me and give me what I needed and craved?*

Wait a minute, I thought, my mind waking up to the company I was sharing. This was Jonas Crane, not just some guy at the bar. And even though some sparks flew between us, he was at most being a gentleman. I needed to behave and not make a fool of myself by attempting to flirt with him.

I took in a short breath, "I think we both had our fill of drama for the evening." I stepped further away from him, and got the strange impression he let me. "I apologize for bringing you into this. I enjoyed our conversation. I just don't want to further impose…."

Jonas eyed me speculatively. "I'll have my driver David take you home."

"You can't. Arch has a car service; I live all the way in Jersey—"

"My driver will see you home," he said cutting me off. His authoritative tone didn't leave room for challenging. No doubt a glimpse of the man that was a leader in business and beyond, and I fell right under his command and stopped.

He reached his hand inside his suit jacket and removed a cellphone, at the same time, lightly clasped my arm as if assuring I wouldn't run off. Not at all like Declan's tight grip, more so a gentleness in it. A warmth filled me as I glanced over him, and his stance in front of me. Apparently, I wasn't going anywhere without him.

CHAPTER FOUR

"**D**AVID IS OUT front ready to take you to Jersey City," Jonas released my arm.

I rubbed my hands over where his fingers had just been, bereft from the loss of his touch. "You didn't have to hold me captive. I wasn't going to run away."

He eyed me speculatively. "No. I suppose not," he said softly. He placed his hand along my lower back and guided me out of the hotel. When we arrived outside, we stopped in front of a black Bentley.

I glanced at the open door and muttered, "Oh the milk of human kindness."

"What thou art promised. Yet do I fear thy nature is too of the milk of human kindness," he replied.

My lips parted. "You quote Macbeth?"

"Yes. But I hope you don't share Lady Macbeth's sentiment," he said and winked.

I flushed. "No. Sorry. I think compassion is honorable. I … I don't know, I ramble when I'm uncomfortable."

His lip twitched. "You quote Shakespeare when

you're 'uncomfortable,'" he bemused.

I shrugged and gave him a small smile. "Well, sometimes … Thank you, Jonas."

He reached inside his jacket, pulling out a card and handed it to me. Four phone numbers. Two for New York, and two for Texas.

I pressed the card in my hand and noticed he hadn't moved away from the door. Was he waiting for something? I stared up at him.

Jonas arched a perfect brow. "Your phone number?" he mused.

My eyes widened as my pulse sped up. Jonas Crane wants my phone number? It was akin to getting asked out by a crush. A toothy grin spread across my face. *Calm down.* I rattled off my number and he programmed it into his cell phone. I covered my mouth.

"I wish I could ride with you," he said. "But I have a call in an hour, and an early yoga session with my ex and my son Paul."

"Yoga. Another hobby?" I asked, my brow raising.

He nodded and leaned against the door. I clasped my hands in my lap to try to hide my trembling. "The ride home is really too generous. Thank you."

Jonas leaned down close to me as if he was breathing me in. "You can pursue me for Arch again," he said in a low rumble that sent a shiver through me.

He brushed his lips against my cheek.

The kiss on the surface was innocent, but didn't match the potent heat coming off his body. My body answered with my own wave of lustful longing as an ache swelled between my thighs. The more he lingered, the less innocent my thoughts became and what might happen with this man who was proving himself irresistible.

His breath trailing over to my ear. "I didn't mean to do that tonight. But you needed a kiss. Didn't you?" he said just above a whisper.

I cast my eyes down and moved a tiny bit closer hoping he would kiss me again. He didn't though. Instead he stepped back and straightened his blazer.

"Good night, Ms. Salomé." His tone was all-professional, like he was addressing a client. Not a woman he just kissed and had me second guessing our time together this evening.

I lifted my chin and averted my eyes. "Thank you, Mr. Crane."

His driver David closed the car door. I glanced out the window and found Jonas still there, watching us until the car entered the street.

Jonas was a danger just as Gregor warned me. I was naïve to think otherwise. Some people are too hard to resist, and he was a force majeure. So opposite from the ruthless, private businessman renown to the financial world. Undeniably alluring though approachable, engaging and charming. He was diverse, even able to engage on anthropology and quote Shakespeare. He captivated my mind after spending only a little time chatting with him. And then he kissed me.

His touch enlightened my senses and left me wanting more. Jonas had me believing in those moments; he understood me wanting to be touched, kissed, and gave it to me. But then at the end, he was professional and reminded me what our encounter meant to him, business. Jonas was and is truly well out of my league, but he was still willing to discuss business with me.

Shaking my head, I leaned against the window as we drifted back across the river to Jersey City. Trying to dispel any thoughts of a possibility with a man like Jonas, but I found it difficult, as I doubted I would ever forget my encounter with him.

We reached my loft apartment on Grove Street in Jersey City and the driver, David, insisted on seeing me to my door. Once we made our way to the fifth floor and over to 508, I thanked him for the escort, and unlocked the door to my apartment, sighing in relief. Something I did every day when I walked in. One of the best parts of living in Jersey City, I found, were the spacious apartments.

The loft had the typical vaulted ceilings and track lighting standard to a lot of apartments in the area. I had added two large black and white framed architectural prints, a blue modular couch, and two modern yellow chairs. I liked the two steel floor lamps Natasha brought with her, and the flat screen TV. Even with the few Sci-Fi and Art photos on our white walls, our space presented more like a "renter's showroom" instead of a cozy home.

I walked a few feet to the kitchen and took out a bottled water, placing it on the gray granite counter. I had worried when I first moved in the white finish in the integrated kitchen would be hard to maintain, but the gloss finish had made it easy.

I headed straight down the short hall to the bathroom to wash off my makeup. I was brushing my hair when my phone went off. My brows rose as I stared at the screen, Gregor? At 11:39 p.m.? He never called me this late. I shook my head and laughed a little. I touched the screen and answered the call. "You can't wait to see how your protégé did tonight?"

"Yes. So tell me what happened. Did you meet Jonas Crane?" Gregor asked.

I twirled the ends of my hair. "Thanks for that, I appreciate it. Yes. I did and he suspected right away I was a stalker of some sort. So I told him about Arch."

"Did he mention me?" Gregor asked.

I bit my lip and sat down on the floor. He didn't mention Gregor, but his facial expression wasn't exactly kind. I didn't want to upset this man I respected though. "I mentioned you, but he didn't comment."

Gregor didn't say anything for a few moments. "Then he remembers me well. So, you're home now. How did he leave it?"

I sighed. I hated disappointing him, but the task he gave me wasn't something accomplished easily. "He gave me his card and said I could pursue him again for Arch."

He snorted derisively. "I just bet," he quipped.

I licked my lips. "He was a gentleman. He even had his private car take me home. Nothing happened." *Except he kissed me.*

"My thoughts are directed at Crane, not you. I'm stressed. Arch is doing better, but small houses get crushed every year. Without a rainmaker like Crane, we may close. What do you think of our chances with him?"

I ran my hand through my hair. If I lost this job, what would I do? Not too many companies were recruiting an Anthropology major with just shy of two years' experience. I could be starting over at twenty-five. "I don't know, but I have his card to try him again," I promised.

"That's the spirit. Just play it slow, let him lead you. Men like Crane like to take charge. Give me an update when you have it."

My mind replayed Jonas holding my arm while he contacted his driver to take me home. Yes. He does. "Will do. Thank you," I said and hung up.

I stared at my phone. *Was I ready to do whatever it took to seal the deal?*

I didn't like the idea of compromising myself to get business, but after meeting Jonas, I had to admit having sex with him wouldn't be a hardship. *Not that he's even interested in sex with me.* And even if I did, who was to say he would go ahead and sign with Arch? How would I feel about myself if he did?

I let go of my thoughts and finished brushing my teeth. Opening up the cabinet, I considered taking sleeping pills. Too much had happened tonight that I knew I wouldn't be able to fall asleep right away. But then an antidote from my father came to mind and had me closing the door. 'Salomé's don't depend on easy fixes. Drugs are easy fixes. Not solutions, Lily.' *I'll try on my own.*

Crossing the hall, I walked inside my bedroom. Opening the mirrored, double doors of my closet. I placed my dress in my dry-cleaning bag, putting the rest of the garments in my hamper. My phone chimed. Declan. *No thank you.*

Seeing Declan engaged only six months after our three years together made my stomach flip. All my traveling back and forth from Quincy down to New York to see him. Time I should have spent with my parents, had I known they would be gone. As for Jonas, he lived out of a suitcase and was based in Texas. Statistically, long distance relationships fail.

With that in mind, I put my phone back down and went to my closet, taking out my black tank top and Boston University black and red shorts. I changed into them and climbed into bed and waited for sleep to come.

Truly, I didn't want to waste time on what-ifs. And I surely didn't want to allow my mind to wonder about a potential client and the possibility of long distance heartache. Still, when I settled down under the covers, I couldn't stop my mind from replaying my encounter with Jonas Crane.

His touch, and his kiss.

CHAPTER FIVE

KNOCKING. INCESSANT KNOCKING at my door. I peeked through my long lashes at the large window along my wall. The sky was still mostly dark with streaks of light in the distance. Natasha.

"Come on, Lily," Natasha called out. I turned over and spotted my roommate standing in the doorway. Her body, built like an athlete, all tone with no curves or hips to speak of, mocked me as she said, "Time for our run."

"It's too early. I'll go to the gym later," I grumbled.

Natasha pursed her bow mouth lips, "It'll only take forty minutes."

I stared at the ceiling. "For you. It's cold outside," I whined.

She held up a knit headband like the one she wore around her long ponytail and gloves. "You can borrow my other one," she said.

When I didn't respond, she continued, "Lily, you're less fat now. If you want to keep looking better, you work at it."

Her words stung, but worked as they often did with

me. Natasha had the body I was bombarded with daily by magazines and on television. I found her body shape elusive, but a goal nevertheless. I shed the "finals fifteen" I gained in college. Fat, spoiled princess. The words echoed painfully in my mind.

I jumped out of bed into my jogging pants, sports bra, white T-shirt, and sneakers. I pulled my thick black hair into one big ponytail.

"I'm not talking an hour, just a short jog along the waterfront and back," she said. "You can go to the gym tomorrow if you like."

Natasha didn't have to offer concessions, but I found they eased her ambush on me. I followed her onto the concrete sidewalk in front of our building and gazed across the water at the skyscrapers of New York City. I couldn't help but think, *there is beauty here too*. Jersey City had become my home over the last two years, but my job in Manhattan was the reason I remained.

Puffing my way back to the apartment, my run had taken an hour and fifteen minutes to return to our loft on Grove Street. When I walked inside, I was pleased to find Natasha already out of the shower and immediately stripped off my clothing and climbed inside.

Once finished in the bathroom, I changed back into my tank and shorts and fell back into bed to sleep.

My phone went off sometime later. The sunshine burned on my eyes as I opened them. My body felt stiff as I lazily climbed out of the bed and down to the floor. I stared at the screen. It was my best friend from college,

Mary. "Hello?"

"Do you remember the book on systematic economic dislocation and socioeconomic deprivation from Dr. Stamford's course?" *Typical Mary!* I thought in admiration ... manic about her academic research. I lived for these exercises.

An academic neuron in my left prefrontal cortex jolted. "*American Apartheid*, the book that discussed the creation and continuity of marginalization and segregation?"

"Thank you. I wanted to quote a few phrases for my paper. Just horrible," she said and puffed. "So when are you coming back to Boston and back to academia where you belong?"

I grinned. "I will only return if they make a new Star Trek TV series."

"You should be getting your Master's Degree in Sociology with me at Boston College," Mary said. She had been trying to talk me into going back for months, but after the difficult time I had finding a decent job with my bachelors in Anthropology, I had decided to pass due to the cost and Declan's chiding on the 'uselessness' of the pursuit.

After experiencing such a difficult time trying to land a job in Anthropology, I would hardly disagree. But of course, I had thought I would be married and starting a family by now. "Declan is engaged," I blurted out.

"Already? Good. I always feared you would go back to the bum. The universe has blessed us. Praise be to all gods and goddesses," she said. "Oh wait, that means some other poor soul is with him. Give me her name so I can do a casting away ritual to send him away from her."

I snickered. "Heather. He was denying the engagement in front of her, so I don't know what will happen."

"Good. I'll just celebrate you're not going back then," Mary said.

I sighed. "Declan wasn't always like that. He had a hard life. He had to take care of his family when his father left. He created his business from the ground up. And, he handled everything when I couldn't manage after my parents' death."

"He was the only one you allowed to handle everything and he was a jerk about it all, too. He was no prince and he broke up with you. That's enough for me to hate him," Mary said. "And I truly loathed him."

I clicked my tongue and turned on my side. Mary's reaction was the reason I started censoring what I shared with her about my relationship with Declan when we were together. The few times I accidentally shared something negative that happened, she grabbed ahold of whatever I shared with her and tried to convince me to leave him. It became unbearable to speak with her. This was the reason I never shared with her the few physical fights we had and worked on them on my own. In truth, I wasn't willing to let him go. Nevertheless, I couldn't argue her assessment on our relationship. His offers to help educate me on life had started kindly. Following their deaths though, they became more severe. If I asked for help with my move, find a new place, stay with him until I found a job, he told me I needed to learn not to "be the spoiled princess" my parents had molded me into.

"Enough about Dec. I stalked a gorgeous businessman last night," I blurted.

"Never a dull moment in New York City. So, what happened? Did you tear your clothes off and jump on his back?"

I laughed. "Hardly. I do love your active imagination, though I reckon the front would have been more satisfying."

"Obscene words from a pristine girl," Mary said.

The Breakfast Club movie quote made me giggle. "I'm not that pristine. I was with Declan."

"Limiting yourself to Declan makes you one. So, please. Yes, you are," she said briskly.

I laid back on the bed. "You keep talking like that, I won't tell you." She mewled and I laughed. "Fine," I conceded. "Black hair, kind of GQ. Chiseled features, Rutger Hauer's eyes or close to tropical, depending on the light. Perfect arch to his brow, tan and tailored, and takes good care of himself."

She sighed. "Sounds like a bit of an Adonis. That's plenty, but what has you worked up?"

I grinned. "He understood anthropology, could discuss philosophy, and quoted Shakespeare."

"Be still my heart. So did half the guys in college. Tell me, what else is it?" Mary pushed.

I covered my face. Mary really understood me so well. "He actually wanted to talk to me about … me. It was easy talking to him, too. I said things I never normally do. Everything. He just seemed caring, kind and, well, assertive."

"That's quite an impression from one night. So when do you plan to jump on him?" She asked. "Wait. He may be the dark and dangerous type; I'll send you some BDSM books to get you prepped."

I laughed. "Geez, Mary … I don't … he's not. I doubt he's like that. He's older, a family man."

"So is my Hans. He's a good fifteen years older than me. And may I remind you he's a vigorous, kinky scholar."

I giggled. "How could I forget?" I recalled the time I ran into our college apartment and found him in a leopard G-string stalking her. "Besides the fact he's based in Texas and a potential client. He's out of my league."

"You're beautiful, Lily. I wish you could see that," Mary said quietly.

"Even if that were true," I paused. "There are plenty of beauties out there and he still could be a client."

"What about Gregor?" Mary asked. "That never stopped him."

I bent my pillow under my head. "Yes, it did, and that's one of the reason's he's divorced now."

"Yeah," Mary said quietly. "He must be freaking out. Sending his girl out to pasture."

I rolled my eyes. "Not this again. I'm not his girl.

You met his latest the last time you were in town, I think."

"He doesn't keep them long enough for me to meet them," Mary said. "And it doesn't make him any less crazy for you." The call waiting beeped.

"I should probably get that. Phone you later, Mare Bear?"

"You better. Tiger—" I pressed the call waiting as my heart constricted. I didn't like anyone calling me by my nickname, at least not anymore. "Hello?" I said gruffly.

"Did I catch you at a bad time, Ms. Salomé?"

My mouth fell open. *Jonas.* "Mr. Crane. I just woke up. I mean, I was up before, I went jogging." *That's right. Impress him with fitness.*

"Jogging? I usually just go to the gym," he said. "You're dedicated."

I laughed. "Hardly, I have a roommate that insisted. How was yoga?"

"Just Hatha, no Tantra," he said.

My cheeks warmed as I suppressed a giggle. "I wasn't serious."

He chuckled. "I think I have your blush planted on my memory. Yoga went well. Even Paul couldn't deny it." He sighed. "How do you feel after last night's news?"

My insides warmed. "I'm okay. More surprised after three years together, I didn't expect him to get engaged in just six months apart. I think I was in shock, but I'm alright now."

"Happens that way sometimes. Glad you're alright,"

he paused for a moment, contemplating. "I was wondering if you would like to have dinner with me on Monday at the Waldorf. We can continue our conversation."

A flutter went through my stomach. Kiss or the conversation? Either way, I wanted to go. "Yes, what time?"

"6:30. I'll send my car to Arch," he replied.

I licked my lips. "I'll take a taxi, thank you."

"You're stubborn. I'll change that," he said.

I beamed. "Good luck, Mr. Crane."

"I enjoy a challenge, Ms. Salomé." He cleared his throat. "David will pick you up at Arch and I'll meet you by the clock in the hotel. 6:30 p.m."

A thrill shot through me. He was insisting. "I ... Okay."

"That's better," he said lightly. "See you Monday."

My face ached from the width of my smile as I thought on the tingle that went through me at his praise. "See you then. Thanks."

Placing the phone down, I stretched out on my bed and let out a shriek. Jonas Crane asked me out for dinner! *No. He asked you out for a work dinner, silly.* Either way, I was thrilled at just the chance to spend time with him again.

CHAPTER SIX

GREGOR STROLLED UP to my desk on Monday morning with a grin on his face. "Guess who's been invited to the Island after all?"

Squealing with delight, I jumped to my feet and hugged him. Arch had been trying to get invited to the exclusive Nile online publishing conference in the Hamptons, but had been shut out as only the top seven and a few small houses were ever invited to their private promotions and exclusive offers.

"Lily," Gregor said with a feigned scowl as he hugged me back, and released me when I pulled away.

I beamed at him. "Congratulations, Gregor! How did it happen?"

Gregor folded his arms. "I'm not so sure myself, but I got a call today and an invitation to attend, and of course I won't refuse, even if it is on short notice." His eyes lit up. "This could mean … God I don't even want to say yet what this could mean." He frowned.

I jutted out my chin. "You won't jinx it, and with Soul Sorrow, Bliss, and Quinton's Memoirs, all at the top of the bestsellers, not to mention all the rest of our library doing well, they would be foolish to snub Arch."

He reached out and squeezed my shoulder. "That's what I needed, a Salomé' special pep talk. Well and...."

I grabbed my notebook and started scribbling. "And I'll start writing Arch's announcement and send it over for your approval. Anything you need my help with? What about your flights? Agenda? I could get some of our PR marketing packages put together to take with you."

He stroked his chin. "You are a wonder. PR has started...."

"But I'll go give them a hand," I said.

"They have covered the flights and hotel. I'll just need a ride to the airport, which I can arrange on my own," he said.

I arched a brow. "I'll get the car service."

"Nope. I'll take a taxi," Gregor said shaking his head.

"Déjà vu. I just had this same conversation with another man," I said. As I moved to past him, he clasped my arm.

"With who?" Gregor asked, his brow lifted.

I titled my head up. "I've got news as well. Mr. Crane invited me for a work dinner tonight and practically ordered to pick me up," I embellished.

"When did he call you?" Gregor asked, crossing his arms.

"Saturday. He wants to discuss Arch with me over dinner." I turned back to my desk and opened my Word document file.

"You know, if you want, I could easily get Mia to go over for the closing part—" he said.

I shook my head. "No. It's too late. Besides, I would like to go."

He blew out a breath. I turned around and frowned. "Everything alright?"

"Yeah," he replied with a smile that didn't quite reach his eyes.

I sighed. "I'll be ok. Don't worry."

He licked his lips. "Okay. But tell me immediately if you're not."

I nodded at him, then sat down and went to task. Completing the draft letter in record time, I ran over to the PR department and put together an extra fifty packages, along with extra media packages for Gregor. I was purposely distracting myself so I wouldn't obsess over my pending encounter with Jonas.

I understood Gregor's reservation better than I had before, though I didn't have a way to block out Jonas's charm or charisma. His kiss alone had me reeling, craving more. So the most I could do was put my worries away and focus on work. Before I realized it, the day had gotten away from me. By the time I checked my watch, it was ten minutes to six.

Wringing my hands, I took inventory of my clothing and hair. My pinstripe suit was wrinkled, there was a run in my cheap nylons, and the chignon I styled my hair in this morning was askew. In all my excitement, I didn't realize until I arrived at work that I forgot to bring a change of clothing. Not only did I look a mess, but I hadn't gotten everything done I wanted to prepare Gregor for his conference. *I can't go like this. Perhaps try to reschedule for tomorrow?*

I didn't want to cancel, but I didn't want to hold up his time if I were to work another hour or two. Or was I delaying? *At least an extra day would give me a chance to dress up, relax and prepare,* I convinced myself as butterflies fluttered behind my ribs. Pulling out my phone, I took a deep breath before calling Jonas Crane.

After two rings, he answered. "Hello," he answered in a low sultry voice that made my pulse quicken.

I touched my face. "Hello, Mr. Crane. It's Lily Salomé."

"Yes. My driver should be downstairs now. You're on your way?" he asked.

I touched the bridge of my nose. "I thought to check with you on possibly rescheduling our dinner for tomorrow?" I stammered. What was it about him that had me stumbling over words when I spoke to him?

Jonas let out a breath. "Unacceptable. I expect you downstairs in my car and in front of me in approximately thirty minutes," he said in a low tone.

I gaped at the phone, rendered speechless.

"You'll need to leave now," he said as he hung up.

Still holding my phone, I thought, *Jonas Crane just hung up on me.* I covered my smile.

"What are you doing?" Gregor asked as he approached my desk. He startled me.

I raised my shoulders. "I was going to try to work a bit more here, and reschedule with Jonas—"

He pressed his lips together. "You can't do that. What were you thinking?"

I swallowed. "I just wanted to get some more stuff ready for you—"

Gregor lifted his chin. "I'm more than ready. You did enough. Now go before I change my mind," he said.

I sighed. "I'm going." I reached over and turned off my computer and glanced down at my creased pinstriped suit. "Jonas insisted."

He squinted. "No man likes to be toyed with, Lily."

I grabbed my jacket and put it on. "I didn't mean to toy. I just wished I wasn't such a mess."

Gregor tucked an errant curl back into my bun. "I know. You're nervous, but just know you're perfect."

I scrunched my face. "Hardly perfect." I sighed, quickly packing up my things. "Thanks for that, Gregor."

We walked to the elevators and through the lobby. Once outside, I turned and said, "Don't forget to save the honey roasted peanuts from your flight for me."

Gregor's lips quirked. "I wouldn't dream of forgetting."

I waved at David and walked over to the car, climbing inside and leaving Arch for the Waldorf. And Jonas.

Arriving at the hotel just before 7:00 p.m., my pulse raced as I stepped out of the car. I hastened my step past the doorman and through the lobby until I made it to the lavish carved bronze clock with a miniature Statue of Liberty at the top. I didn't know how I had missed it before. It was beautifully positioned in the luxurious lobby, as was the man standing next to it. Jonas Crane.

My body hummed as I moved closer to him, undoubtedly his complete opposite. Confidence and authority exuded from him. Still, he was standing there, among the many admirers gawking at him, waiting for me. For me? A thrill went through me. This incredibly gorgeous man wanted to spend the evening with me. *For work.*

Jonas looked striking in a charcoal gray two-piece suit. His impossible sea blue eyes bore into me upon approach, making me flush as they roamed over me assessing. He came close to me and tucked my hair behind my ear and a tingle went through my body on contact. My skin heated as I thought about my creased suit under my gaping coat and running nylons. I had hoped to be looking more at my best for my next meeting with him.

My head dipped before him. "Sorry about the call. I didn't have enough time to change and I forgot to bring an extra set of clothing for tonight. I didn't mean to stand you up. I just didn't want to appear…." I gestured my hands down at myself.

His lips turned up into a gorgeous smile that caused a flutter in my chest. "Hello, Lily. Glad you made it."

I took in a short breath and smiled back at him.

"Hello, Jonas. Thank you."

"We have reservations at Peacock Alley. But if you'd prefer, we can have it sent to my suite where we can relax and chat?" Jonas asked.

I nodded. "Yes. Ok. I'd like that."

His hand moved to the small of my back and led me towards the elevators.

The door closed and the small space filled with him. I peered down at his Italian leather shoes in front of me. The sleeve of his suit brushed against my arm. I took in a shaky breath.

"Nervous again," he said, amusement in his tone.

I nodded as I played with the buttons on my coat.

He reached his hand inside my coat and fixed the lapel on my suit, smoothing the fabric in place his gaze steady on me. His palms brushed my breasts. "We'll relax, eat and talk. How does that sound?"

Did he do that on purpose or was he just being helpful?

I tucked my chin under as my face heated at the timbre of his voice and the possibility that he felt or could see my nipples hardening at his brief touch. I wasn't sure, and was too embarrassed to ask, so I worked against my pounding heart and staggering breath and said, "Sounds great."

Once out of the elevators, his hand slipped to my back once again and guided me toward the entrance of his suite. Opening the door, he waited for me to go inside first. Crossing the threshold, I was astonished by the dimensions and opulence before me. The foyer had exquisite marbled flooring and opened to an elegant seating area. There were large rose petal rugs situated under two antique loveseats and a highly polished mahogany coffee table that had a welcome basket and a bottle of champagne poised in a silver bucket. Next to the dining table was a fully stocked wet bar.

Jonas opened a door next to where we stood and removed his jacket and shoes.

"I'll take your coat and shoes," he said, placing his hand on my shoulder to assist me out of the coat.

I groaned as I wiggled my toe, eyeing the hole in my nylons when I took off my heels. "They are a menace."

"You may take those off, too," he said, peering down at them with me.

I may? *Odd,* I thought.

"A glass of wine, Lily?" he asked as he headed over to the bar.

"Sure," I called out. I absently reached under my skirt and yanked along the top and started to pull off my nylons.

"There is a bathroom to the left."

I turned in mid-motion, connected with Jonas's face. His gaze was dark, and I froze in place under its weight.

My blush burned my face. "Excuse me." I quickly eased my skirt back in place, darting into the bathroom and closing the door. *Why did I do that?* My brain had abandoned me. Jonas completely unnerved me.

Gazing around the bathroom, I marveled at the décor as I removed my nylons. It had an open-seated vanity area with an oval mirror and full-sized complimentary toiletries. A mini-chandelier hung from the ceiling, complete with gold light sconces and satin covers, and the black and white patterned marble flooring glistened under my feet. Further inside, I admired the huge marble tub with ornate fixtures and a pedestal sink with mirror. I splashed water on my face and freshened my mouth in the sink.

As I moved back to the door, I saw an open closet with terry cloth robes and slippers. *Let them eat cake, indeed.* I was delaying, but I couldn't hide out for the whole evening. He didn't see anything, just an awkward bend and my hands grappling under my skirt. I *can face him again*, I prepped myself.

Leaving the bathroom, I put away my nylons and then turned around and gazed over the large living area.

I stood next to the couch and tried to curb my dreamy expression as Jonas leafed through a leather bound menu. He had removed his suit jacket and was now in his dark slacks, his white shirt unbuttoned at the collar. He glanced at me and patted the seat next to him.

"Have a seat. We'll order together," he said.

Right on cue, my stomach growled. Sitting down a little further over than his instruction, I attempted to view the menu by leaning over. Jonas turned and studied me for a moment, then moved his arm up along the back of the couch.

"I won't bite, at least not right now." He winked at

me.

I laughed, and eased closer until my pencil skirt brushed his trouser leg. Inhaling deeply, I caught the incredible fragrance of his cologne, but that wasn't the only distracting thing. His dark hair and almost turquoise eyes were striking. Combined with his chiseled features he was, as Dee would say, exceptional.

He brought the menu closer. "What would you like to eat?" he asked.

My face fell as Declan's words filtered through my mind. *You lost some. You're still a fat spoiled princess.*

"I usually don't eat too much at night," I said ignoring the lowering of his brows as he stared at me. "Maybe the infamous Waldorf salad, and a Mezze Platter?"

Jonas shook his head. "That's not enough food for dinner. You'll eat a proper meal," he said dryly as he flipped to the entrée section again. Apparently he wasn't letting this go, and he had invited me to dinner, so I tilted my head and bent to the task of searching the menu again.

Jonas tucked a curl back in my bun and smoothed my hair in place. "Do you like chicken? Turkey? Beef? Fish?" he asked.

My breath hitched. *Should I be letting him do that?* He just did what he wanted. It unsettled, yet intrigued me. I could feel the heat of his body so close and tried to suppress the shiver that went through me.

My pulse sped up as I timidly pointed to a seafood selection. "I like them all. I love Sea Bass."

"Good. Grilled Sea Bass and Waldorf salad," Jonas muttered. Before I could respond, he rose and walked to the phone and ordered a Sea Bass and salad for me and a steak for himself. He also added two deserts, a truffle cheesecake and chocolate cake. When he turned back around he caught my scrunched face and grinned.

"Just in case you're still hungry." He winked.

I smirked back at him. Charming and intimidating.

Jonas returned to the couch and sat down facing me. "Let's get back to where we left off, you grew up in Quincy, completed your Bachelor's Degree in Anthropology at Boston University, work as a publishing assistant at Arch. But you wish you were working as a cultural researcher or doing some philanthropy project for the disadvantaged."

My face lit up. "You remember all that?"

"My memory is holding up well," he said evenly. "How old are you?"

I smirked. "You're not that much older than me. I'll be twenty-five in a couple of months."

"That's twelve years younger than me." He titled his head up.

"It's just a number," I said. "Doesn't mean anything."

Jonas's mouth curved up. "We are not only different in age, but in circumstance."

My shoulders dropped. I was still reaching for my dreams, and he had already achieved his. "My parents were different in age and circumstance. My father was twenty years older than my mother."

"Is that so?" His brow raised. "What did your parents do?"

I licked my lips. "My father was a principal viola player for the Boston Symphony and my mother was a first grade teacher at Marymount."

"What happened?" he asked. "If you don't mind my asking."

I stared at my hands. "They were killed in a drunk driving accident. Well, I don't necessarily consider drunk driving an accident: the killer chose to drink and drive…." I said bitterly.

His face held warmth and empathy. So much so, I felt tears threaten my eyes. I averted my gaze and attempted to gather my senses. *Not now.* "It was years ago. I'm fine."

Jonas frowned. "You have more family?" he asked, clasping my hand.

I swallowed against the lump in my throat as I stared down at his hand holding mine. "No. Can … can we please talk about something else?"

He started rubbing soft circles on the back of it and I would have given everything I had for him not to stop. "We can, if you'd like," he said.

I shrugged. My mind went completely blank.

"Paul, my son, is a prodigy pianist. He's at Julliard," Jonas offered.

"That's great. My father was a child prodigy in violin and viola. You must be really proud," I said politely.

"I am," Jonas' eyes clouded over. "I only wish I could say I had been around to help him cultivate it. With work, I'm in New York, if I'm lucky, twelve days a month. Less when he was growing up."

I squeezed his hand.

"He's fifteen now, and, well … a handful. No longer easy. I regret that." He turned his ring.

I glanced down at his hand then met his eyes. "Why do you wear your ring?"

He offered a weak smile. "Now you moved into a subject I don't want to talk about."

My head tilted down. "I'm sorry. It was none of my business."

"I didn't want the press to know my private life," He gripped his knees. "And to be honest, it feels like I failed. I guess removing the ring makes that failure real."

I placed my hand over his and added a light pressure. His earnest, raw confession touched me. I met his eyes and saw a sadness that I wanted to somehow chase away. But I had no idea if I could, so instead, I offered whatever assurance I could. I moved further still until I was against his chest. He wrapped his arms around me.

"I never said that to anyone, not even to Dani." I could hear the surprise in his voice.

Gazing into his eyes I said, "It's part of our conversation. I won't tell anyone."

Jonas leaned down and kissed me. His mouth moved over mine with smooth and firm expertise. As quick as it started, he broke the kiss, and searched my face as I panted in his arms.

Whatever he found had him seeking my lips again, this time with urgency. He swept his tongue inside my mouth and slid it against mine in a teasing caress that I felt down to my core. My breasts swelled as I pressed against him, my own desire and need seeking more from him. A moan rose from my throat, and he answered with his own as he held my face and continued our kiss.

The door chimed, and a voice called out, "Room Service." Breaking away, he gently smoothed my hair and back. The air shifted between us and I could sense his reservation.

"We'll talk more after dinner." He stood and walked over to the door, and I traced my fingers over my lips, a tingle coursing through my body. His kiss had the taste of more.

Standing up, I made my way over to the table as the waiter walked out and closed the door behind him. Jonas held out my seat for me, and I thanked him and sat down.

Once we were both seated, he held up his glass. "I always start a meal with a toast, so please indulge me," he said. "'What is a man, if his chief good and market of his time be but to sleep and feed? A beast, no more.' Having you here is a pleasant hiatus from the monotony of my work. Thank you."

I lightly tapped his glass and beamed at him. "Hamlet."

"Yes." He took a sip of his drink. "You, Lily, give me

hope for the youth of today."

I rolled my eyes. "I'm hardly a sample of the youth of today. My father used to say 'all Salomé's must have a fine grounding in arts and literature.' He used to assign me homework growing up."

"I like that, and wish I had done so with Paul. But he's too much like me. He's a rock lover. Beatles and Led Zeppelin are the only ones in his collection I can listen to."

I laughed. We ate in silence for a few moments. I found the grilled Sea Bass to be heaven on a plate. The salad was equally delicious.

"I love the Beatles too," I finally said.

"My all-time favorite songs are Maybe I'm Amazed, Something, and Women. All so beautifully crafted. The words are so honest and raw. They say I'm afraid. I'm imperfect. I love you with all my heart." I was babbling.

I met his eyes and flushed, "Sorry, I tend to ramble."

"You're fine. I'll also take a road away from time to time," Jonas replied, his tone light.

"I have a great fondness for that song and that love. You're a romantic," he said.

I dipped my head and smiled. "I suppose I am." I glanced up and found his eyes on me.

We ate the remainder of the meal in a comfortable silence. The food was one of the best meals I had in a long time and my belly appreciated every morsel by me clearing my plate.

"I see you were hungry." Jonas smirked at my clean

plate. "Would you care for dessert?" He ran his hand through his hair, giving me one of his winning smiles.

My face fell as Declan's comments on my eating habits came to mind again. *Never full. Always packing it away eh, Lily?* "I'm stuffed, truly, thank you."

"You alright?" Jonas touching my arm. "Did I say something?"

I shook my head. *He* didn't. "Sorry. It was just a thought. I'm fine."

Jonas sighed. "You're not. Come here." He tugged my hand until I stood and pulled me into a hug, which I took, molding my body against him. His body was solid muscles under his shirt and as I inhaled, my nostrils filled with his incredible scent. He was truly intoxicating. What was probably a minute seemed longer, and when we parted I would have given anything to be in his arms again.

Nevertheless, we cleaned up and stacked the items on the cart. Afterwards, he escorted me back to the couch to sit down.

"Now, for the next part of our evening," Jonas began, suddenly formal. "Did Gregor send over a copy of the proposal with you?"

Work … of course. I stood and walked over to my bag and removed the proposal. Handing it to him, I sat back down.

His gaze stayed on my face as he flipped to the back page and signed. "I'm agreeing to place Arch Limited on the short list for presentations to me in six weeks. A space left for the top three I'm considering to publish my book."

My jaw dropped. "Wow. Seriously?! Wow. Gregor, my boss is going to be over the moon!" I exclaimed. "Thank you, Mr. Crane. I will go and call him now and—"

"Wait." Jonas placed a hand on my arm and I sat back down. "There's more. But Arch's agreement has nothing to do with what I wish to discuss with you next." He rose and refilled our drinks and handed me a glass of wine and sat down facing me.

"As you know, I travel for work. And as I said earlier, I'm in town for about ten days a month. I'm divorced. And you are single?" Jonas asked.

I nodded and took a sip of wine. "Yes. I am."

"Do you have friends in the city?" he asked.

I shrugged. "Not really. Well, I do have my room-mate, and my boss. But my best friend Mary lives in Boston. We try to see each other often, but with graduate school…."

"So no one you spend time with here?" Jonas putting his glass down and waiting for me to answer.

I licked my lips. "Well, I guess Gregor. He comes over for my silly old movie marathons, with a few acquaintances, but no one I'm dating or seeing much of."

"I know you went to the symphony. Did you enjoy it?" Jonas asked.

I nodded a little. "Yes, I did."

Jonas paused. His gaze intent as he placed his arm along the back of the couch. "Are you lonely?"

My eyes darted over him, but I kept my mouth closed, not sure if I wanted to answer.

"I know I am," Jonas admitted, his hand running through his hair. "Dani has moved on. She has Alan now, and my son Paul is busy with friends. I'm finding myself alone when I come back here. I have friends, but it's different."

I ran my hands down my arms. "I can imagine. With Declan, his friends were friendly to me when I came down to spend time with him; but when we broke up, my friendships with them ended."

Jonas reached out and lightly clasped my hand and let go.

"Lily," his gaze bore into mine. "I would like to see you."

My pulse sped up and I clasped my hands together. "See?"

"Yes. I hate going out alone. We'd go to the symphony, the opera, and various engagements. Basically going out in New York with me."

My mouth went dry. "I. I don't know what to say? Why me?"

"You're beautiful, and easy to talk to. You're smart and unassuming." His lips curved. "The rest I go with my instinct."

I moved my hair in front of my face to hide my smile. *He thinks I'm beautiful?* "So like … dating?"

Jonas blew out. "Not exactly. I'm not ready for a relationship. It would be more like companionship." He took a sip of his scotch.

My brows knitted. "Companionship like friendship?"

"Well, we are acquaintances now, and with our conversations, I hope we develop a friendship. But companionship is not solely friendship."

"What would make this companionship different?" I asked.

"Sex," Jonas said bluntly. "I want to have sex with you as well as spend time with you."

A clenching low on my body had me shifting in my seat and a silly grin spread across my face. *Jonas wants to have sex with me?* Should I be flattered or offended?

"You alright?" Jonas lightly touching my shoulder.

I jumped in my seat. "Sorry." Lost in my thoughts, I hadn't realized I'd been quiet for a few minutes.

"I won't bite you. At least, not yet," he said in a low rumble. The exact same words he said earlier in the evening. The heat of his gaze left no doubt the words and his intent were deliberate.

My breath hitched. I touched my warm cheeks as my mind imagined seeing the body of the beautiful man next to me. My face fell as I thought of my own body and Declan's words to me. *You've a pretty face, but your body….'* "I don't see how you could or would want that. You haven't really seen…."

"I do. I've thought of little else since Friday," Jonas said candidly.

My face turned to hide my delight, and polished off the rest of my wine.

Jonas reached out and steadied my hand as I returned it to the coffee table. My mind struggling to comprehend Jonas's confession, and offer to me while my body heated wanting to take what he was offering.

Sex. His choice of words sunk in further. Not love making. *This wouldn't be dating, he said companionship.* He wanted something like a business arrangement. Would I want to do that or would I feel used?

"What would it involve?" I asked. "Besides the … sex," I said just above a whisper and blushed.

Jonas tilted his head, a ghost of a smile on his lips. "It could be like tonight, dinner and conversation."

I frowned. "Just … like that. Meet for sex like a contract escort?"

Jonas shook his head. "No. Just a verbal understanding between us. This is not transactional, but if there's something you want, I'd be open to getting it for you. As far as sex, only when you're comfortable with me. I've been tested recently and I'm clean. I can give you the information, but this arrangement, this companionship, would involve you being available for me."

My face scrunched. "You don't even know me. How could you be so sure? I mean, I'm on the pill." I took a glimpse of him. *Smoking hot.* "I've only had Declan as a sexual partner, and was tested after we broke up because I suspected he was cheating, but yeah, I'm clean." I babbled. I clasped my hands over my mouth, but my sex life and lack thereof, spilled out. "God. What am I saying? I can't do this."

He looked away and brushed his hands down his face. "You're innocent. I can't do this with you."

I crossed my arms. His words bothered me. Perhaps it was my Salomé' ideals overtaking my insecurities. "Ha! Now you think I'm not worldly enough to be your friendly companion?"

"You just said you didn't want to do it anyway." His hands tunneling through his hair. "And yes. Your lack of experience is a concern of mine."

I pursed my lips. "You were married for sixteen years," I quipped. "That hardly makes you a Don Juan."

Jonas eyed me as a mischievous smile appeared on his lips. "Well, since you brought that up. We had a poly-amorous time in the earlier part of our marriage. I wasn't innocent before that either." He chuckled and shook his head. "I can't believe I'm even discussing that with you."

I pursed my lips. "You want to share me? No way."

"Sharing was something Dani wanted, and I was open to it as well." His gaze swept over me. "No. I won't share you." Jonas reached his hand out and stroked under my chin. "You'd be mine. My companion."

My heart pounded in my chest. He said the words with conviction, and I couldn't suppress the thrill that went through me at the thought that he would want me all to himself.

Jonas eased his hand away and sighed. "Please leave this in our conversation. I'll have David return you to your home, and as I said, Arch is still on my short list so you can share that with Gregor Worton." He lifted the paper for me to take. "I'm sorry if I offended you."

Averting my eyes, I made no movement to reach for the document. "Is this because of my lack of experience in bed?" My shoulders hunched.

"No. In a way, your inexperience sexually turns me on," he said frankly. "What I'm not sure about is that you'd be able to handle just companionship. I don't want to hurt you."

I sucked my bottom lip. He still wanted me in and out of the bed to spend time with him. But there would be nothing beyond friendship. Could I do this?

His gaze dipped to my lips and flicked up at me, making me catch my breath. "I do want you to agree," he said softly.

Jonas reached out and wrapped his arm around my shoulder, pulling me against his side. The feeling was akin to being wrapped in a warm blanket. Small and safe in his arms. Allowing me a taste of what he would give me. I wanted to remain, but he let me go, and sat there awaiting my input.

I was to decide where we would go from here. A gorgeous powerful man wanting to take me out when he was in town was more than I had now. He said he was lonely.

I was lonely too. I had no family and my best friend lived in Boston.

The possibilities of Jonas taking on Arch took the weight off my mind on work and paved the way to a possible promotion that I may have earned on the press alone. Knowing Gregor, he would be over the moon brimming with ideas on ways to expand Arch. The money from the promotion could also help increase my sponsorship for the Salomé' Love Legacy. Who knows? Spending time with Jonas could give me contacts in the cities to participate in the week.

I wanted to say yes, but as Jonas pointed out, what about me personally? Could I handle being basically his fuck buddy?

Then again, a chance to be touched, to be desired, was more than I had now. And it was something I had only had for a brief periods with Declan. *Well, until he found me sexually unappealing.* This would also remove any chance of my falling back to Declan when I was lonely … or when I couldn't stop my thoughts and grief. A chance to explore myself. See if life beyond my first lover was possible. Why not at least try?

I didn't want to leave. Right or wrong, I wanted this.

So, I met his gaze and said evenly, "Could we try?"

"Yes," Jonas said without hesitation. He exhaled and leaned back, studying me. Reaching out, he trailed his hand down the side of my face. "I have work to do, but we can start by collecting your things and having you stay here."

My eyes dilated. "Stay here for how long?"

"I leave Friday," Jonas said. "It will give us a chance to get better acquainted and to see how this works between us."

I glanced at him. "Have you done this before?"

"Yes," he said, but didn't elaborate.

My mouth turned down. I wasn't sure if I wanted to know that I might be one of many.

"Okay. I think that'll be fine. But I can go back on my own and return."

Jonas took my hand and leaned over close to my ear. I held my breath. "Going to your place gives me a chance to get to know you," he said gingerly. "If you'll excuse me," he stood, "I need to make a call, and then we will head over to your place."

"Okay," I said. I walked over to the closet, pulling out my own phone. Glancing over my shoulder, I met his gaze still on me. I felt a tightening low in my body at the thought of what I had just agreed to try with him.

Sex with him. My mind raced ahead and I sought a moment to myself. Taking my phone with me, I went into the bathroom. I wanted advice, but I didn't really know what I would be able to share. I decided to call Gregor and at least inform him about the news for Arch. His phone went straight to voicemail. Still, I left a message.

"Jonas signed the proposal and has placed Arch on the shortlist of publishing companies that will get to give a presentation to him before he announces his choice. I knew you would be excited to use that publicity at the conference. Talk to you soon." I tried Mary next, but again got voicemail and hung up.

I splashed water on my face and dried it. Pinching

myself, even though I knew this was real. Jonas wanted me as his companion. I searched myself and already knew the answer. I wanted him too. Whatever happened, I wanted to try and see if I could handle such an agreement. Drying my face, I rejoined Jonas out in the hall and we left the hotel for Jersey City.

CHAPTER SEVEN

J ONAS TOOK MY hand and held it the second we sat
down, even though he remained on the phone until we
reached the Holland tunnel. His effort was comforting
on the outside, but didn't ease the jitters inside me. This
only escalated to sweating when we were less than a block
from my apartment. My thoughts raced on my place in
comparison to the Waldorf suite. My plastic and metal
frames, the Star Wars posters lining my walls. What
would Jonas Crane think? Hell, his designer clothing
probably rivaled the cost of everything I owned. When
the car stopped in front of the renovated warehouse, my
heart pounded so hard the sound filled my ears.

I chewed my lip. "I could just run inside," I said softly.

Jonas didn't respond verbally, but helped me out of
the car and followed me inside the building. He was
coming with me whether I wanted him to or not. I blew
out a breath as we took the elevator and fumbled with
my keys as I unlocked my front door. But Jonas, ever the
gentleman, held it open and motioned for me to walk in.

"Nice apartment, Lily." Jonas gave me a soft smile that melted my insides.

"I'll hurry," I called out as I started running towards my bedroom. "Make yourself comfortable."

"Or you could come back here," I told him. No. I wanted him back here. Running back into the living room again, I found Jonas still standing where I left him when we walked in. "Do you want to come back here?"

"Yes," Jonas said and laughed hardily as he strolled down my hallway into my bedroom. He appeared to fill the space, such was his persona. As I danced around him collecting things, he captured me and cupped my face in his hands, causing a rush of heat to join the jitters I already had at having him there.

"We will be going out the next four nights. You need to pack one formal dress, yoga pants, a T-shirt, heels, lingerie. I'd like to see all of them," he said.

I dazed for a few seconds. He was being quite specific, but I assumed this was part of the companion agreement. So formal, like a business plan. *A sexy business agreement,* I reminded myself. I exhaled and went over to my closet, taking out my college backpack as well as my silvery V-wrap around dress. I also grabbed the black faux wrap shirt and one of my business skirts, bringing them over to my bed. Then, I picked up a pair of black yoga pants and V-neck T-shirt from my dresser.

Jonas stared at each item and a soft smile appeared on his lips. "I like your choices. Now your undergarments."

My cheeks warmed. I exhaled as I brought over the black lace and pink satin sets that were the best I had, and reluctantly walked over and placed them down on the bed. "I don't really wear that much—"

"I wouldn't want you to wear them with me," he said evenly. "But I'd like to see them on you at times."

Hot! I thought as a smile broke across my face and a tingle went through me. He was being sexually direct, though with a bit of charm and I was finding it intriguing. Every innuendo was making my pulse race. This gorgeous man on my bed wanting me was more than I had time to think about. I left the room and quickly collected my toiletries, brushes and placed them in the backpack once I returned back to the bedroom. Jonas was walking around perusing my Star Wars and Star Trek posters and video games with an amused grin on his face. *Well, this is who I am,* I thought.

Stopping in the doorway on my second trip, I found Jonas seated on my bed holding my hardcover of *Peter Pan*. He was smiling and shaking his head.

"You need a proper bag." The left corner of his mouth turned up.

I shrugged and zipped my backpack. "I can dress casual at the office, and it would be a waste to over-pack for a couple of nights. I'll carry a garment bag for the dress and skirts."

He chuckled. "Ever the vagabond, Tiger Lily," Jonas read aloud. The inscription was from my father to me. Their nickname for me. I faltered, swaying a little on my feet and biting my lip hard as memories surfaced.

Jonas crossed the room and wrapped his arms around me from behind. "Come here." He guided me to the bed and held me in his arms, "Talk to me."

I took in a ragged breath as I struggled to stay focused and not give into the pain arising in me. *Why is this happening?* I had managed so long without faltering, but with him, I was having a difficult time doing it. Maybe it was because he seemed genuine in his query about me.

Taking a deeper breath, I closed my eyes and settled in the warmth of his arms. "Tiger Lily. My dad loved J.M. Barrie's Peter Pan stories and would read them to me over and over again. My parents told me I was a beautiful princess like her. They treated me like a princess." He stroked my back and waited for me to continue.

I struggled to talk through the ache in my throat. "I wanted to be her, braiding my hair, trying to dress like her. So my father gave me research projects and taught me to study Native American culture. That led to more study projects and ultimately, my passion for cultural studies in college, and the Perchance to Dream, that art exchange program I worked on with my mother until her death. Well, I still help run it now, but they renamed it to 'Salomé' Legacy of Love.'"

"Salomé' Legacy of Love. Tell me about it." He positioned me to lay in the crook of his arm, as if he had all the time in the world to listen to me.

I nodded. "I know it's a small piece and all the negative stereotypes and biases in the work, but for my parents, for us, it meant something different. My mother encouraged me to be carefree, and my father encouraged me to be brave. Both great qualities of a Tiger Lily princess, they told me." I choked. He wiped my eyes with the back of his thumbs.

I licked my lips. "Well. It's an art week where artists around the area come to teach their art to students in our teaching district. The proceeds help students that can't afford to get art supplies and instruments. It also links them to mentors that periodically check in to give them encouragement. I had expanded it to satellite groups in Kenya and Brazil. My dream is to make it a real cultural exchange, where we can send students and they can send artists for a week. With ongoing social media contacts, I'm hopefully raising enough money for scholarships … I don't know."

His lips parted. "Tiger Lily's life bloomed quite brightly in you."

My heart contracted. "I don't really like anyone calling me that anymore." I swallowed as he gripped my hand. "They were the last words I heard from my parents, as they left the night they were killed. It's a reminder of what I had and lost. I won't be a Tiger Lily again."

Jonas didn't say a word, but reached for me and held me against his chest. Tracing small patterns along my back, I drank in the comfort of his arms. I don't know how long we stayed like that, but he didn't seemed concerned. As my heart settled, I eased out of his arms, with a slight tug. Had he wanted or needed the same comfort?

I smiled at him. "Thanks, Jonas," I whispered.

He cleared his throat, "Send me some information about your project."

I frowned. "It wasn't my intention to pitch it to you I just thought … well, companionship is sharing … right?"

"It is what we make of it." He lifted his chin. "I find you interesting and therefore what catches your imagination, also interesting."

I shrugged. "Okay. I guess."

We brushed lips. He tasted of Scotch and mints. Our kiss slowly grew more passionate and I opened my mouth and he slipped in with a hard tongue. His mouth explored me, smooth, firm, tangling with my lips.

I wrapped my arms around his neck and tried to pull him down on me. He stopped me, pressing me down on my back.

"We keep this up, and I won't be able to keep that promise of waiting," Jonas said.

I didn't make that promise. Jonas must have read the reaction on my face and chuckled.

"I'm glad you're finding it difficult, too." He cupped my chin up to him. "There is something I want."

I smiled up at him. "Yes?"

Jonas eyes deepened in carnality as they lazed over

my body making my pulse quicken. "You unclothed. I want to see you naked."

I managed to hold onto my smile, as I cringed inside. What he wanted was not necessarily unreasonable. After all, if we had sex he would see everything anyway. Yet my mind thought about the bright factory lights of the space, and the gorgeous man on the bed next to me.

What was I going to do? I walked over to my halogen floor lamp and twisted the knob to a soft setting. I then walked over to main light in the bedroom.

"What are you doing?" Jonas removed his jacket and sat down on the side of my bed with his arms folded, his facial expression befuddled.

I flicked the light off, leaving us in a dim lit room. "I'm creating mood lighting."

"Where I can't see anything?" he said dryly.

I stared down at my bare toes. "It's too bright in here for that," I said meekly.

"Come over here," Jonas commanded, his arms held out to me.

I reluctantly crossed the room.

Jonas pulled me closer to stand between his legs. "You're face went sad again. What's wrong?"

I'm afraid you will be repulsed by me. My mind started playing instances in my past that support that theory, but Jonas's squeeze on my hand brought me back. "I'm not comfortable in full light, and, well, now you probably want to go. So…."

"Don't tell me what I'm thinking," Jonas said abruptly. "I want to understand. Is there a problem with me seeing your body? Do you have an ailment or…."

I shook my head. "I'm just uncomfortable…."

Jonas took my hands and studied me, then kissed my knuckles. "Okay. That's fine, Lily." He let go and lifted his suit jacket. I sat back on the bed and hunched over. He surprised me by picking up my backpack and garment bag. "David will be downstairs to take us back to the Waldorf."

My eyes widened. "You still want me to come?"

"Of course. I'm eager, but not impatient," he said, winking at me. "You're uncomfortable, so I will wait for you."

A small smile formed on my lips. *He'll wait.* "Thanks."

He leaned down and kissed my forehead. "I need to see, touch, and taste every inch of you. And I want you to want me to do that," he said in a low voice.

His words were meant to titillate, and my body responded to them by sending pulses of pressure down to my core. A moan escaped my mouth as I squeezed my thighs together.

Jonas gasped, his gaze raking over me. He put down my things and gripped my waist to still me. "You need me, Lily?" He sat down on the bed and pulled me between his legs. "You need me to touch you, make you come?"

My breathing became labored as my heart hammered in my chest. My mind battled with my body as I struggled to think under the warmth of his hands, now on my hips. "I … we … should wait," I said breathily.

"Why?" Jonas asked, his hands sliding against the fabric of my skirt to cup my ass just before he squeezed.

I could feel my pulse in my throat as I tried again to gain control of my senses. "It's not right. It's too soon…."

Jonas didn't answer, but his breathing wavered as he eased a hand down the length of my skirt, then up between my legs where he gripped my inner thigh.

My head fell forward, meeting his. His touch on my thigh had me parting them more as a moan escaped my lips. "Jonas," I rasped.

Jonas moved the fabric as he inched his hand a little higher. "Let yourself go," he whispered.

My pulse was in my throat as heat coursed through my body. I could feel my arousal pool between my thighs. "Please," I mumbled.

Jonas reached the apex of my thigh and stopped. "Open your blouse," he ordered, his tone low and rumbled.

My hands trembled as my fingers fought to unfasten the three buttons on my suit, exposing my breasts in my white lace bra, my hard nipples pinched tight in the fabric.

Jonas let out a groan. "You didn't want me to see you?" His tone was mockingly admonishing. He leaned in and pressed his head against my breasts and I gasped. "You've got me ready to come and I only saw your bra," he said huskily.

My eyes shuttered as I moaned and arched against his mouth as his tongue traced around the pinched peak of my nipple and sucked through the lace of my bra. He then turned his head and I whimpered, desperate for him to continue.

His hand moved further up my leg to rest at the elastic band of my panties. "Tell me to do it."

"Please," I whispered.

Jonas tilted his head back. "Look at me."

My lips parted, and a jolt went through me as his dark gaze and tight jaw filled my vision. I could see he wasn't lying. He wanted to give this pleasure to me, and that knowledge only made me hotter. I moaned loudly as his fingers slid under the fabric against my wetness.

"So wet, so hot," Jonas hissed. He tightened his grip on my waist then slid his finger through the slick flesh of my sex, expertly stimulating me. I was feverish as the pleasure filled me.

"Tell me what you want," he commanded.

What does he want? How can he think? I whimpered and wanted more of his finger, and sought to move to get it, but he held me tightly in place.

"Please don't stop. I. I need," I said incoherently. He added another finger, pushed them inside me, and moaned against my breasts.

"Your pussy is sucking my fingers." He pushed them in and out of me rhythmically, running his thumb over my clit. "You need this. Tell me."

My skin heated to boiling as I started riding his fingers. "Yeah, yes, I need you touching me, inside of me."

"Touch you where?" Jonas said in a low tone.

I felt myself unravelling, as the orgasm he built in me grew closer. "Between, my legs," I stuttered.

He chuckled then dipped his head and closed his lips around my nipple and sucked as he stroked my clit. Thrusting faster with his fingers making me shake hard in his arms.

My limbs stiffened and I cried out as the orgasm crested and exploded over me, "Jonas." He tugged harder on my nipple and held me tight, taking every spasm within me. Kissing the space between my breasts, he lifted his head up to me.

"Lily," he whispered.

My eyes filled as my heart pounded in my chest. I met his piercing, dark gaze in his gorgeous face. His desire for me was there. However, as I came down and he released his grip on me, my shame at giving in so quickly so soon after his offer engulfed me.

I closed my eyes and muttered, "You must think badly of me.…"

"For letting me give you what we both want?" He nuzzled my neck as he slipped his hands from under my skirt. "There's nothing wrong with getting and receiving pleasure."

A tremor went through me as he lifted his fingers, coated in my arousal, to his mouth.

He ran his tongue over them and sucked. "Just a

taste, and I want more." His eyes flashed at me.

My face burned as I stood there, unable to answer or move in this moment.

He squatted down in front of me and pulled my panties down my legs, and off.

I waited for him to hand them back, but instead....

He lifted his chin as if challenging me to ask for them back and placed them in his pocket.

"Why would you want to keep them? I mean...." I stared at him in disbelief.

Jonas gave a wicked grin. "You find that odd after I just finger fucked you and licked your wetness off my hands?" He gave me the same stare back.

My skin felt like it was on fire. "I ... Okay."

Jonas laughed outright. "Oh, Lily, I delight in the more I learn about you."

CHAPTER EIGHT

I WAS HAPPY that I didn't have to speak again during the ride back to the hotel. Jonas received a call and talked on the phone the whole way there, occasionally moving to rest his hands a little higher on my thigh. Truthfully, I couldn't blame Jonas for the sexual tension that had settled between us. After I practically begged him to touch me, he seemed assured he had found his new companion. He not only made the offer, but found out pretty quickly he could order me to do as he wished when he touched me.

It was a vulnerability that exposed and shamed me. Declan had learned it too, and took advantage of it until I repulsed him by gaining weight. I still wasn't as thin as I was when I first met him, but Jonas's facial expression seemed genuine and the bulge in his pants left me with no doubt he was turned on by me. What I found puzzling was that he hadn't sought pleasure for himself.

"We're here," Jonas announced, breaking my thoughts. His hand took mine to help me out of the car. He had David carry my bags and I meekly followed them back up to Jonas's suite.

Once we were alone again in the room, he immediately headed for his desk and opened the top of his laptop, pressing the on button.

"You can hang up your clothes in the closet or the bedroom through the far door," Jonas said as he moved over to his desk.

Choosing to put my things in the hall closet, I turned around and found Jonas was now wearing a pair of glasses. I ogled. *Wow. He's a sexy Clark Kent.*

A smile played at the corner of his lips. "You alright?"

"Yeah," I said, nodding emphatically. That earned me a grin from Jonas. He didn't seem to mind my gawking at him. No smugness, just pure confidence on his face. No doubt comfortable with getting this reaction from people all the time. After all, he was, indeed, scorching hot.

I fidgeted. "Um. Would you mind if I take a bath in that huge tub?" I asked.

"No. Make yourself at home," Jonas replied.

I turned, then looked back and bit my lip. *Were we having sex later?* I wondered in shock that my mind had readily accepted the possibility. "I usually wear a tank and shorts to bed, just so you know."

A smile played on his lips. "You can wear them tonight."

What I'd wear beyond tonight hung in the air. I couldn't blame him for the change in his expectation of me as I myself had the same expectation. The thought of being naked in bed with him had my body humming again. I squirmed.

"You need me again, Lily?" Jonas folded his arms.

Yes. "No. I'll just go relax in the bath," I said absently as I sucked in air. Why did I say that? I scolded myself and turned away. *What am I doing?*

"Don't touch yourself," Jonas called out behind me.

I stopped and turned my head back, as heat flooded my body. I stared at him, his shoulders rising and falling with his breath.

"If you need to come again, you bring yourself to me," he said in a low tone that I felt right down to my core.

I glanced at him and asked, "Why didn't you?"

He lifted a brow. "Why didn't I what?"

My skin burned. "I could have … You could have," I stammered.

Jonas smiled broadly. "Why didn't I have sex with you back there? I wanted to see your response to my touch. And it pleased me."

"Oh," I said the only thing that came to mind and turned toward the bathroom.

"Oh, Lily," Jonas called out, "you won't have to wonder long."

I quickly turned back and went inside the bathroom. Closing the door and pressing myself against it. I may have nodded to him. I didn't know, but what I *was* sure of; his words aroused me. I felt the pang of desire coiling within me. I was aching with need again, and he had offered to help me. So why was I in here?

The answer was there as slipped off my clothing. Jonas gave me the touch I craved, but on his terms. After all, he presented the offer, and stimulated me to orgasm in my bedroom. Sure, I didn't have to show him my body, but he still had me show him something, and admit to him what I desired. In truth, Jonas was already controlling me sexually. Did that bother me? No. I wasn't aggressive and never initiated sex with Declan, though I never turned it down either.

Stripping off my clothes, I glanced down at my body. My heart constricted as I recalled the first time Declan had showed me how to create the mood lighting that made me "look better." It wasn't long after that when he added viewing porn as a "warm up." *Oh how I wished I looked better.* I washed my face and brushed my teeth while I waited for the tub to fill for my bath. In the vanity, I found lavender body salts which I added to the water. I then shut off the nozzle and sunk in the warm, scented water and relaxed. The soothing aroma calmed my jittery nerves.

After a while, I heard Beethoven's *Pathetique* waft through the bathroom door. I imagined my father playing it on our upright in our house on Franklin Street, always after my mother and I begged him, wading through his sighs and critiques of his own playing. My heart swelled as it progressed to the second movement. She would wrap her arms around him and kiss his cheek, then pull me into a hug and kiss. I tried to breathe as sobs erupted in me, struck by the realization that I would never experience that again. What was this? I felt cracked open.

"Lily." Jonas knocked on the door.

I wiped my eyes and swallowed hard. "One moment." I pulled the curtain in place and stuck my head out the side. "Okay."

Jonas stood in the doorway, looking devastatingly handsome. His dark hair was finger-parted across his forehead, his lean, muscular frame on display, along with a hint of smooth chest hair along the Vee of his T-shirt. His brows lowered. "Are you crying?" He stepped inside.

I waved a hand around the curtain, then wiped my eyes and managed a weak smile. "I'm fine. I. I love this sonata and it always makes me weep in its beauty. If sorrow had a voice, it would be *Adagio Cantabile*, it's … perfect."

Jonas stepped further inside and leaned against the vanity. "Don't be afraid to share your thoughts. I so enjoy them."

I eyed the lights. Though not as bright as my bedroom, they were still enough to make my heartbeat accelerate. I looked down at the absent bubbles as I tried to focus on what Jonas was telling me.

"Beethoven wrote this when he was twenty-seven for Venetian Prince Karl von Lichnowsky, who was a patron of Mozart as well. If you are moved by *Adagio Cantabile*, what do you think of Mozart's *Sonata K*? Are you familiar with Jan Ladislav Dussek *Sonata in C* minor?"

"Yes, I'm familiar with Dussek. I did play the violin for a while when I was younger, but it wasn't in me," I said.

"I played the guitar in my youth, partly as a defiance, and because I wanted to be Jimmy Page. But borrowing your words, it wasn't in me."

His gaze was salacious when he met mine again. "I should leave you to your soak," he said quietly, but instead advanced to stand near the bathtub. "But I don't think you want me to."

"Jonas," I said huskily, my voice giving away the desire I had for him. The heat of his stare made it hard for me to breathe. I didn't. I wanted a hug, a caress. I wanted more. He walked over and stopped next to the tub, the curtain the only thing between us.

I drew my legs up and held them. My eyes darted to the lights and raced with all my insecurities about what Jonas would see if he pulled the curtain, the last barrier.

He touched the curtain. "Let me see all of you, Lily."

I closed my eyes. He wasn't repulsed in the bedroom, I told myself. "Oh ... okay," I stammered.

Jonas slowly eased the curtain back and sat down on the edge of the tub. Reaching over, he lightly tugged away my hands. I let them drop down, revealing my breasts.

My face burned as I forced my eyes to meet his and was met with a lustful stare I felt down to my toes. My heartbeat sped up and the pulsing throb between my thighs had already made up my mind for me as I took his hands and gingerly stood up.

He drew in a sharp breath. "Oh, Lily," he said hoarsely.

Before my mind could break the charge between us, Jonas bent down and crushed his lips to mine. He wrapped his arms around me, molding our bodies together. I could feel his erection pushing hard through his pants—the only thing between us. When we parted, our breath was coming in heavy gasps. I blushed in my nudity and the soaked front of his clothing, but Jonas didn't seem to mind.

"You're beautiful," he said with conviction. Then he reached his hand for mine and I clasped it as I stepped out of the tub.

Jonas handed me a towel and I turned away from him and started to dry off. I felt another towel brush against the top of my shoulders, moving down my back. Jonas was helping me, and though I found this unusually intimate, I didn't try or want to stop him.

My breathing was short as his towel slipped down my backside, where he halted. A moan escaped my lips as he replaced the towel with his bare fingers, sliding over my buttocks.

"Your skin is so smooth, so soft." His tone was barely a whisper. He moved the towel down the back of my thigh and legs, at the same time using his hands, creating a trail of goose bumps along my naked flesh. I dried my front, but the whole time, I was tuned to Jonas as his fingers moved over me. Even after I was dry, I was wet and ready; wanting, needing, whatever he would do to me.

Jonas didn't stop me as I cinched the towel at my waist, but took my hand and led me out of the bathroom. Though my mind was already running ahead, our pace was slow, as if he was waiting for me to tell him to stop what we were about to do together. I felt as if I was barely holding my head above water with him.

We didn't stop walking until we entered the bedroom. I stood in awe of the sleigh bed in front of me, of the gorgeous ivory embroidered duvet and pillow set that contrasted the ornately carved dark oak frame.

Jonas seized my lips possessively. "I'll be right back." He then walked out and left me burning in the room, staring after him.

I sat down on the bed and fussed at myself. I lacked all decorum, going as far as allowing myself to stand naked before a man like Jonas Crane. Still, he found me beautiful.

But was I ready?

CHAPTER NINE

THE SOUND OF the door opening sent my heart pounding. Jonas entered the room, naked, revealing his incredibly toned lean muscular body and washboard abs. He had a smooth expanse of hair on his chest that trailed down his body. He was bold and breathtaking.

My gaze dropped lower to the impressive girth and length of his engorged cock. The sight sent a sensual flush through me. I felt my nipples hardening as they swelled and wetness between my thighs. I trembled on his approach.

"Nervous?" Jonas asked. His brows rose as he sat down next to me and pulled me against his side.

I nodded. "I want this. Believe me, I do. I just want you to be … I don't know."

His eyes shuttered and a small smile appeared on his lips. He reached out his hand and stroked the side of my face. "Lily, don't worry. I'm already pleased. In fact, I'm honored."

I covered my warm face. "That's not exactly what I mean."

He pulled my hands away and lifted my chin up to him, studying my face. "I know what you meant. One thing you will find is that I prefer to take over."

I sighed long. I was relieved he understood what I wanted from him. "So, what now?"

Jonas gave me one of his wicked smiles. "Now? Sex isn't a commentary, Lily."

He leaned over and kissed my mouth. His lips moved over my face, and down my neck and collarbone. I returned his kiss with desperation, as all my needs crashed over me. I reached my hand between his legs and delicately trailed my fingertips around the smooth hardness of his bulging erection. He groaned and covered my hand with his and eased it away.

"Relax. We'll get there." He moved me to my feet before him and tugged off my towel, tossing it on the floor. I flushed as his eyes roamed over my body, igniting everywhere they fell. His hand trailed between my breasts and slowly down to my mound.

"Don't hide yourself from me again," he said in a low, authoritative tone. "You're beautiful and sexy." He reached out and pulled the covers back. "Lie down." I climbed in the bed and rested on my back. He swept away my hair, which was covering my breasts, and looked down at me. He took a deep, cleansing breath and reached for my hand.

"Keep your eyes on me, and breathe."

I hadn't realized I was holding my breath and exhaled. He took me through it a few more times, until our breathing synced.

Jonas settled next to me on the bed and started to kiss me again. He then moved down and began to massage me, starting with my legs. As he moved his large hands up to my thighs, I felt wetter, hotter. I quivered as my body swelled, wanting his hands to touch higher.

"Breathe." He moved to my hips. All the time, his eyes were fixed on me, studying my responses to his touch. He moved past my belly to my shoulders.

I whimpered, "Jonas, please."

"Soon," he whispered. I ached, but fought my frustration and tried to stay focused on him. The sight of Jonas's hands covering my breasts, the feel of his hands kneading them, made my breathing shallow and my pulse quicken. I arched against him. *More.*

"Deep breath." I breathed as he pinched my nipples, scraping them with his teeth then gently nipping. I moaned, arching up and moving my hands through his hair. He let out a groan as he suckled and massaged them with soft licks of his tongue. He then eased my legs wide apart and settled between them. I was so turned on; I could feel my arousal on my thighs.

Did he feel it? His eyes stayed connected to mine. His hand slowly caressed down my breasts and over my stomach, followed by his lips. He kissed and ran his tongue over my belly button and a shiver went through me. He parted my legs wider and moved further down. My body hummed and the throbbing pleasure between my thighs became almost unbearable. "Jonas."

"Bend your knees and open your legs," he commanded, the tone of his voice just above a whisper. My pulse was in my throat as I timidly moved into the position he wanted me in. I was so exposed to him.

His hot gaze swept over me. He gently rubbed my thigh as though to soothe me.

"You're glistening, beautiful."

I held my breath, wanting him to touch me there. But Jonas only lowered his head and stared. My breathing became ragged as I tried to remain still. He pressed his hands on my thighs and leaned over and inhaled, "Mmm ... I'm savoring this."

I closed my eyes as he moved down further, his shoulder against my thighs poised for oral sex. Something I'd tried twice, but had never felt overly comfortable with.

"I can't come that way," I whispered.

"Look at me," Jonas said, calling me back to him. The look he gave was challenging and I suppressed the annoyance inside from spreading to my face. It was just a lot of pressure added to our first sexual experience together.

"I want you to relax and feel." He ran his fingers through my soaked labia and circled my clit. A shiver went through my body as hunger darkened his face. He bent down slowly and replaced his fingers with his tongue. I jerked as the sensation pulsed through me. His tongue was hot against me, and his sensual soft licking had me arching up to his mouth.

"Mmm," he hummed. He breathed me in and I shuddered, struggling to take in air. I looked down at him and his eyes were steady on me as he slid his tongue inside, in and out, then back up to circle my clit. I felt my orgasm start to build within me, but the newness held me back, along with my own thoughts, and I lost it. I was sure Jonas would give up, but he kept at it, licking slowly upwards, upwards, until my orgasm was building again. I stroked the silky strands of his hair.

"Jonas, it feels. So … God. Thank you, but—"

Growling, he started sucking ever so gently on my clit, and my mind left as though he'd flipped a switch.

Gripping my thighs and steadying me, he pushed in his finger and crooked it inside me as his tongue pressed and sucked me relentlessly.

"Jonas," I yelled out as the orgasm wracked my body. I gripped his head tight, allowing the vibrations to pulse through me, moving and pressing myself against his mouth as orgasms exploded over me, breaking me apart, and I thought it was the end. But Jonas was unyielding in his attention and his mouth stayed on me.

Gripping my ass as he buried his face deeper licking and sucking me. I cried out and moved to end it, as the sensitivity was more than I could bear. I couldn't get away though, as wave after wave of climaxes vibrated through my body, jerking me against him. He pushed me for more than I ever had before, and held me to him until everything shredded inside me, leaving me empty, floating in utter bliss. It was only then that he willingly let me go.

"Look at me," Jonas demanded. I raised my watery eyes to his face, utterly speechless. I started to shake and he moved up and wrapped his arms around me as I calmed, holding me against him and kissing over my cheeks and forehead.

I reached between his legs and tried to stroke his shaft, but he took my hand and moved it to his mouth, kissing my fingertips. He pulled me on top of him and kissed my lips, sweeping his tongue inside my mouth, filling it with the sweet tangy flavor of my sex. I molded my body as close around him as I could get and closed my eyes.

"Thank you," I whispered.

Jonas kissed the top of my head. He reached up and wiped the tears leaking from my eyes as he held me close to him. My breathing was short as I struggled to stop them.

"Let go, Lily," Jonas said softly. His permission was all I needed and I surprisingly unleashed my pent up pain and grief. He embraced me. Kissing and whispering soothing words as I emptied myself further in his arms.

After a while, I stilled and reached down between his legs, again attempting to stroke him.

"Please, just let me," I whispered to him.

Jonas paused, then relaxed back as I gripped his shaft. I gently wrapped my lips around him and sucked. I tried to gauge how fast, how hard, by his moans. I moved him further inside my mouth ... deeper to the back of my throat.

Groaning, Jonas grabbed my hair, flexing his hips as he moved against my mouth.

"Good … so fucking … good, Lily…." Jonas purred. His head tilted back, his eyes half-lidded. His cock was hard and soft at the same time. His scent, clean and dark. I wanted to explore him, I softly squeezed his balls, and stroked his shaft as I sucked.

I glimpsed up at him as I increased my speed, gliding him in and out of my mouth, moving him further inside, wanting to take all of him.

Jonas clasped my head grunting, as I sucked him and caressed over the soft hair below. He arched and started panting. I moved, licking under his balls, continuing to work him with my hand. Jonas cried out, and I knew he was close.

Moving back up, I started stroking and sucking him faster. "Oh, Lily," Jonas said, barely coherent as he moved faster and I tried to meet his demands, desperately wanting to please him as he did me. Finally, he broke, and came gripping my head tightly as it hit the back of my throat in hot spurts. I swallowed him down, sucking steadily, drinking down his essence. He pulled me back on top of him, gently stroking my back and still breathing heavily.

After a while he said, "You … you are passionate about many things, Ms. Salomé."

I smiled against his chest. "I could say the same about you, Mr. Crane."

Jonas's head turned toward the side table and the time displayed on the clock, 12:42 am. Jonas kissed the top of my head. "We'll finish this tomorrow night." He eased me on the bed. "I'll set the alarm for 7:30 and we'll have breakfast." He helped me to my feet. "My car will pick you up. Yoga pants and shirt, we will be going to the yoga meditation center after work."

I rubbed my neck. "I don't know, Jonas. I don't mind yoga at the gym, but I'm not into all the new age hippy crowd."

Jonas chuckled. "I don't expect you to convert, I expect you to come there with me as my companion."

My chest tightened. He was with me as a companion. *This isn't the beginning of a relationship.* "Okay. I'll be ready to go at 5:30." I was pleased at the evenness of my voice.

"I find the center a great place to relax. We won't stay long." He kissed my cheek. "I plan to spend the rest of tomorrow night inside you."

I licked my lips and gave him a shy smile, then collected my towel and went to the bathroom to clean up. *I'm extremely lucky*, I told myself. *I have a gorgeous man that is attracted to me and interested in giving me pleasure.* My mind worked over the benefits of the companionship. I would get a chance to go around the city again, and have a handsome, willing partner to have sex with.

What more could I possibly want?

I was happy, but I realized it was short lived. My mind didn't work that way and flashed on the tears I had shed in bed and Jonas's strong arms embracing and soothing me. I could tell myself all I wanted that I didn't need a relationship and that companionship was enough for me. Yet there was danger here, and it was in his intimacy and care. Things I wanted and needed, but that could be taken away from me if I allowed myself to get attached. Jonas was clear he didn't want a relationship, which might mean he would move on eventually to his next companion. My stomach turned over as I cinched the towel around me and eased the door open.

Once back in the sitting area, my eyes ran over an incredibly handsome Jonas sitting on the couch in his robe with his laptop in front of him. I stood there gaping until his eyes came back to mine.

"I need to work out a few points for my meeting tomorrow," Jonas said, as if he needed to explain to me.

I took a few steps towards the couch. "Can I help you? Or just stay and keep you company?"

"No. Go to sleep," he said.

Sobering. I started to obey, but then Jonas called out, "Wait." He walked up and tugged the towel down, kissing my breasts and stroking his fingers between my thighs. I half-lidded my eyes as he pulled me flush against his dick, now hard against me.

"Damn it. I can't think with you naked in bed," Jonas gritted. I smiled against his chest, pressing myself closer to him. He sighed long and slowly released me.

"I promise, I won't be long," Jonas whispered.

I nodded, lifted my towel and went into the bedroom. After a while, I sighed and changed into my tank and shorts before turning off the light. *A danger, indeed.* Climbing under the duvet, I curled on my side and eventually fell asleep.

CHAPTER TEN

I WOKE TO the feel of soft kisses on my face. My eyes popped open and my heart stopped when I realized it was a strikingly handsome, tousled Jonas over me. He flashed a grin as he pressed his body down on me. I could feel his cock through his briefs.

"I don't remember you wearing more than a towel when I left you last night." His eyes darkened as they stared down at my tank top, making my nipples harden. I should have been embarrassed, but my body had taken over as heat coursed through me. I moved under him, against his cock, and moaned. Our eyes met and we gazed at each other, his breathing just as hard as mine.

He ended it by kissing me hard on the lips. "If I didn't have to work, I would spend the day on that sexy body of yours." He climbed off me. "But I can't. So you save that orgasm for me."

I grumbled, "Fine."

His lips twitched. "Don't be grumpy. I'll make it up later." He then went about getting dressed, leaving me breathless.

I went to the closet and collected my clean clothes and workbag, then went into the bathroom. I took a quick shower, adding some light makeup and brushing my long black, thick hair into an oversized bun. As I gazed in the mirror, I tried to wipe the grin off my face. I was never good at hiding anything that I was thinking or doing. My parents always knew what I was up to, so I was known to confess pretty quickly. Mary and Gregor too. *Well, most things.* He always noticed every haircut or unflattering piece of clothing I came to work in, making it his business to provide a running commentary. Luckily, Gregor was out of town.

My eyes widened and I reached for my purse. *Gregor!* I remembered I had sent him a text. I picked up my phone and looked down at my new message from him, then burst into a fit of laughter. It was a cat dressed as Lady Gaga dancing to her *Edge of Glory* song. *Well, I guess he's pleased with my message about Jonas.* I walked out the door and put my things away, then sought out Jonas. I found him seated at the table with an assortment of pastries, fresh fruit, and coffee before him.

I walked over to where he stood. My breathing became labored as I allowed my eyes to roam over him on approach. His black hair was styled back, showing off his gorgeous, freshly shaven sculptured face.

He grinned at me, "You look lovely." He leaned over and kissed the side of my face. My nostrils filled with the incredible aroma of his light aftershave. "I have no idea how Gregor gets work done around you."

I covered my grin. *Jonas gives good ego.* My mind wandered back to the previous night, and I turned my head to hide my face. When I finally turned back, there was a knowing smile on Jonas's face.

"Damn it. You keep doing that, I'm going to fuck you on this table," he said.

My breath hitched as I glanced up at him. The look he gave was predatory. I had little doubt he wouldn't do exactly as he said. "I don't know what I should do."

He chuckled. "I know, and I like that," he said softly. He reached out and stilled my hand. "Have breakfast."

I took half a muffin and a few strawberries, placing them on my plate.

Jonas frowning at my plate. "Not enough. Eat the whole muffin and another fruit," he said.

My eyes focused on my plate. "I'm not big on breakfast."

He clicked his tongue. "That's what you said about dinner. Please don't tell me you are starving yourself," he said with added distaste.

I jutted my chin. "No. I just didn't want to load up on carbs. I hate feeling bloated all morning."

He rolled his eyes. "I saw no bloating last night."

I rolled my eyes back at him, then added a banana and the rest of the muffin. I stole a glimpse of him and my stomach fluttered at the wide grin spreading across his face.

I licked my lips. "I'm not doing it because of you."

He smirked, "Yes you are."

I grinned and took a bite of my muffin. "How do you know Gregor?"

Jonas paused for a moment, then said, "I knew him briefly years back." He took a sip of his coffee, and from his demeanor and the following silence, I knew that was all he was willing to share.

I quickly ate the rest of my breakfast, ignoring the groan sent my way by Jonas. We rose and collected our things, heading down to the lobby together. We passed the concierge desk and moved out to the black Bentley at the door. I climbed inside and moved over to allow Jonas to sit down beside me. His driver closed the door and the car left the queue before the hotel and joined the mid-town morning traffic.

Jonas took out his phone and started talking on it the second we settled in the back of the car. My hopes of capturing his attention for a little longer were put away. I stared out the window at the passing cars and the myriad of people heading off to work this morning. It was only Tuesday, and I had only met Jonas four days ago, though so much had happened. He took my hand and held it firmly, yet gently, as it finally registered that we were at the Arch Limited building on East 44th Street. Jonas climbed out of the car and helped me onto the sidewalk.

"Jonas Crane." I turned my head and caught sight of a suited group of men heading our way. I turned back and leaned towards Jonas for a kiss goodbye, but Jonas not only hesitated, he patted my arm. "See you at five thirty." He started moving away from me.

I swallowed hard as I turned my face to recover, hoping he didn't see my embarrassment as I moved away from him, tossing a wave over my shoulder and running inside the office building.

Why did I do that? I worried as queasiness threatened to expel my breakfast. My mind replayed all the times Declan had stood separate from me so no one would think he was with *a girl like me.*

Jonas was way out of my league. And the quicker I understood that, the easier things would be, or so I hoped. Wiping the corners of my eyes, I skipped the elevator and ran up the five flights to our office. I stopped to catch my breath, then pushed through the steel door and walked over to my computer and turned it on.

My stomach soured as I took out my cell and saw two messages from Jonas.

I'm sorry I hurt you this morning. Let's talk about it.

I texted him back:

I'm the one that should apologize. I didn't mean to embarrass you. Sorry.

I rubbed my throat to soothe the ache there.

Don't apologize. We'll discuss this at 5:30.

I pursed my lips. *If I go at 5:30.*

I worked through the morning, though my mind shifted between last night and the morning. I didn't know what to make of the last night, Jonas, or the stranger on the street. Over lunch at my desk, I picked up the phone and called my friend Mary for advice.

"NuqeH?"

I groaned. "Klingon, Mary, really?"

"You need to stay sharp for when you visit over Christmas. Star Trek Next Generation marathon."

I groaned again. "It's January, Mary."

Mary knew I avoided the holidays like the plague, but she had started making Christmas full of things untraditional and coaxed me into coming a few days last year.

"I'll think about it, but I have a bigger problem." I looked around my cubicle, making sure no one was around to eavesdrop. I lowered my tone, "The Shake-speare quoting suit and I had oral sex last night."

Mary giggled. "Hell yeah, but why only oral?"

I huffed into the phone. "It was late after we went to pick up my clothes."

"Wait. What? I'm confused. Start from the begin-ning," she said.

I sighed and quietly told Mary everything that hap-pened from the dinner, to the companionship discussion, and finally the morning kiss denial.

"Maybe he doesn't kiss on the lips. Oh, wait that's not true eh, sex kitten?" Mary said and laughed.

I groaned. "I'm hanging up."

"Okay. I'm sorry. It's new. You need to relax. He said companionship, so he's not ready for kisses at the door and flowers. Just try to enjoy yourself," Mary said. "I don't think he was being like that asswipe Declan."

I twirled my finger around my hair. "You're right. I'm just ... I don't know."

"You like him," Mary said. "Nothing wrong with that. Just think about your own rules to protect yourself if you want. Maybe you both could make a list of rules so you don't rabbit boil?"

I frowned at the phone. "Mary, you're getting close to Natasha now."

She cursed and I giggled. "No way. I love you, kiddo."

"I love you too, Mare. Thanks." I hung up the phone and buried myself in my work.

After running to the corporate gym and working out vigorously during the remainder of lunch, I dragged myself back to my desk with a turkey salad in hand. It quickly became a dry husk by the time I got through the work Gregor had forwarded from his conference.

By 5:15, I turned off my computer and went to the bathroom and changed into the yoga pants and top. I pulled my hair into a ponytail, and added a little lip-gloss then walked back out to my desk where I found my work phone flashing. I picked it up. "Hello. This is Lily."

"About time I reach you. Didn't you get my messages?"

Declan again. I sighed. "You didn't leave messages. I did see you called though. I've been busy working."

"I know you're mad about what happened last Friday, but I don't want Heather. I want you, Lily. I always wanted to marry you and have a family with you."

I tightened my jaw. "I really can't talk. I have an appointment at 5:30 p.m."

"Three years is too long together to throw away," he said, ignoring me.

I turned off my computer and collected my things. Our time together didn't matter when he dumped me. "I really have to go."

"Don't be a bitch, Lily. You're not good at it."

I grimaced. "Calling me a bitch? Now I really have to—"

"—Wait. Please, I miss you. I still use your stuff you did for me at work. I miss talking to you, how you listened and said sweet stuff to me. You still cooking? Remember you and your mother making me treats? My workers still ask about—"

My heart squeezed. He remembered that. My mom and I baking every week and sending cookies and cakes to his work. "I gotta go—" I said nasally.

"—I know you miss how I made love to you. We can still have the kids you wanted. Girl and boy. We'll name them after your parents."

I closed my eyes. *Why did I keep listening?* "Bye, De-clan." I hung up on him and turned off my phone, then shoved it in my handbag. I rubbed my temples in a poor attempt at removing all the thoughts and memories that arose from his conversation.

When Declan was good and trying to get along with my family, my mom did try. But he wasn't towards the end, and he cast me away in a city I moved to for him. It was over, and I wasn't going back.

Running down the stairs, I opened up the door to

the lobby and jogged out the front of the building, where I spied Jonas's Bentley. As I approached the door, Jonas climbed out and the GQ suited man I had left this morning was now in loose fitted pants and a Vee-neck black T-shirt, similar to mine. My heart sped up at the sight of his dark curls and chiseled features. He was really a gorgeous man.

No greeting? Jonas took my bags and handed them to David, who placed them in the trunk. I climbed inside the car and Jonas climbed in after me and closed the door.

Crossing my arms, I asked, "How was your day?"

"Awful, but not from work. Look at me." His tone was authoritative, and I found myself buckling to his demand by turning my head towards him.

I smiled weakly. "It's perfectly fine. I embarrassed you." I felt a pain at the back of my throat. "Can we just put this behind us?"

His facial expression turned stern when he fixed his gaze on me. "I didn't expect to run into one of my father's old friends. He didn't know about the divorce. I didn't want him starting rumors before I had the chance to speak with him. It wasn't because I was embarrassed. Never think I'm embarrassed of you."

I sighed in relief. "Thanks for explaining that to me." I licked my lips. "Okay. But I'm sorry. It was spontaneous. I didn't mean to overstep—"

Jonas reached out and took my hand in his. "Stop apologizing…." His facial expression softened and I felt the initial tension melting away. "I will introduce you next time we see him," he said it as a declaration.

I smiled. "Okay. Thanks." Jonas gently rubbed the back of my hand with his thumb. He leaned over and kissed me softly, lightening my senses.

"Kiss me," Jonas commanded. His gaze locked with mine, and I trembled. So close to him, I was overcome by his beauty. The sculpted angles of his face and sensual pout of his full lips. *My, oh my.* I couldn't believe I was with him, let alone that we had been together intimately.

My heart pounded in my chest as I leaned in to meet his demand, pressing my lips against his. He held back and let me lead. I kissed along his jawline, then moved my hands up to his shoulders, and met his mouth again. When I sat back, I eyed him inquisitively.

He flashed a smile. "I want you comfortable with me." He lifted a brow. "But you want me to take the lead?"

I shrugged. "Yeah. I suppose I do. Is that okay?"

He cupped my face in his hands. "Yes. Like I told you last night, I prefer it." He gave me a searing kiss that left me hot and panting next to him. "Now that we have properly greeted each other, let me take a look at you."

I fidgeted next to him as he lightly touched my hair, the side of my face, and down my neck to my shoulders. He grinned at me mischievously. "You have on a bra. Lean forward." I did as he asked and his hands skimmed up the back and unclasped it. "You won't need one tonight."

My brows furrowed as my hands quickly went under my shirt and I clutched the bra in place. "I never go braless. I'm much too … full. I'd be uncomfortable."

"Not for the yoga we are doing this evening," he said cryptically. He didn't say anything else, but I had the impression he was waiting for me to follow his request.

My pulse increased as I eased the bra down my arms. *I guess this isn't that big of a deal.* I told myself. After all, most of yoga is stretching and breathing. "What are we doing?"

"It's a surprise," Jonas said, his face blank.

I started easing the T-shirt back into place when he tugged my shirt back up. "If you wear it, I can't do this." He leaned down and sucked a nipple into his mouth, running his fingers over the swelling plains of my other one.

"Is that why we're going there?" I said huskily, as I moaned and pressed into him.

Jonas squeezed my breasts in his hands, "Partly, but that will give too much away." His breathing was as labored as mine as he groaned and suckled my breasts.

His eyes darkened as he moved his hands to my thighs and squeezed them. "I wish we had more time." Jonas's hands moved to my hips and stopped.

His eyes widened as his mouth spread into a broad grin. "Panties with yoga pants?" He peeled down the sides of the pants. "Oh, Lily." He let go of me and chuckled.

I covered my hot face. "It's not that silly."

He tugged at my hands and cupped my chin up to him. "No, and I didn't say it to embarrass you." He pecked my lips. "Your innocence just surprised me."

I glared at him. "I'm not innocent. I think I proved that last night."

His gaze bore into mine. "I'd still say you are. Sex doesn't make you impure." He kissed my lips again, then let my face go. He leaned over next to my ear, "You can keep them on."

I giggled and hit his arm, and he laughed. He pulled me close to him and placed his arm around me. I relaxed and we rode down the mid-town traffic to uptown. I didn't know what to make of the yoga center we were going to, or Jonas's ideals of me. Nevertheless, he had somehow made me feel at ease. In fact, I found I liked his playful control of me, though I wondered just how much play it was, and how much he would actually take from me in the end. I pondered this as the car moved through traffic. When we finally slowed and I peered out the window, all I could see was a row of brownstones.

"This yoga center is run out of a house," Jonas said, plucking the query from my mind. The car slowed down and we stopped, got out, and walked up the driveway and down a short flight of stairs. The fragrance of incense met us at the door, along with a small elderly Indian woman in a beautiful white tunic and pants. Her face lit up and a smile formed on her lips.

"Namaste, Jonas," she said.

"Namaste, Padma." He moved me in front of him

and rested his hands on my shoulders. "This is Lily and it's her first time here." She smiled at me and we walked further inside and up to a desk where she wrote my name on a nametag and placed it on my shirt.

"The session tonight is a bit advanced." Her voice just above a whisper. "For couples."

My lips parted. *Couples?*

"I know," he said flatly as he guided me past her.

"I didn't mean…." Padma cleared her throat. "I just wanted you to know Dani is in the other room with … Alan."

His brows knitted. "Oh. Apologies Padma, and thank you."

Jonas moved up a few steps away from her, then turned to me and said, "Dani told me she wouldn't come tonight." He ran his hand through his hair.

His ex-wife Dani? She was here? I understood his reservation and I wasn't sure how this would go, though he did mention they were friendly.

I touched his arm. "We don't have to stay. I'm here for you. We can go," I offered.

Jonas gave me a small smile. "It'll be fine." My tension eased in his assurance. He proceeded by splaying his hand on my lower back and guiding me down a short hall into an open alcove. There we saw intricately carved, built-in shelves marked "shoes" lining the walls. From what I could see, the place was decorated in an Eastern theme.

Brightly colored silks hung on the walls, along with

beautiful tapestries of gods and goddesses. The floors were decorated with mosaic tiles. With the large stone pedestals holding even larger candles, the place reminded me of a temple, though most temples didn't have state of the art kitchens and adjacent cafés.

Jonas stopped moving and I followed his gaze to a tall slender blonde with a pageboy haircut standing next to a guy with round glasses and a ponytail, circa 1967 hippy. The female had an upscale artist air about her. Maybe it was her designer bohemian clothing. Nevertheless, she was a coiffured beauty.

They started moving towards us. Jonas closed the distance and gave the woman a hug and a kiss on the cheek.

"I didn't know you were coming," he said.

I chewed my bottom lip as I looked at the warmth flowing between the two of them. The man touched my arm. "I'm Alan."

"I'm—"

"Lily," Dani finished for me as she moved away from Jonas and leaned in, surprising me by cupping my face and kissing my cheek. "Jonas told me you would be coming with him. Welcome."

Alan touched Jonas's shoulder and shook my hand.

"Thank you," I said softly, moving back to Jonas's side.

"She reminds me a little of…." Dani clicked her tongue.

"Maggie," Jonas answered quietly.

Dani smiled and nodded in agreement. "Yes. Greg's Maggie. But wow, those silver eyes and lips." Her gaze raked me from head to toe. "Makes me wish we ran across her back then." She wiggled a brow at Jonas and giggled. He laughed a little with her.

I let my hair fall forward, and Jonas reached out and tucked me against his side. "Let's not scare her," he said dryly.

Dani beamed as she looked between us. Alan leaned over and kissed her cheek, and she smiled up at him. "We just came for an early meal and chat. How about a cup of chai? Before your class?" She clasped her hands together.

"Okay," Jonas said. He led me to a table, then walked away with Alan to pick up the drinks while Dani and I sat down together.

"You'll have to forgive me. I knew you would be here tonight, and my curiosity got the best of me. So we decided to stop in to meet you," she replied.

I didn't know how to answer so I nodded, then looked for Jonas, and found his gaze was on me.

"She's fine," Dani called out. He just shook his head. "He's afraid I'll say something that will make you run away." She winked. "I don't want you to run away, though. Which is why I recommended this session tonight. Give you a chance to sync your energy together."

I raised my brows. "Like soul and spirit body energy. I read some Eastern Philosophy in college…."

"Yes!" Dani exclaimed, clasping her hands together. "Jonas said you were clever. Now I'm having my own 'Lily' conversation."

I gave her a smile. Jonas had mentioned me to his ex-wife? *That's odd.* What was I doing chatting with his wife about him? I covered my mouth.

"Oh, please don't be uncomfortable," Dani said and grinned at me. "Yes. Jonas did mention you to me. We talk about everything. You needn't worry."

"She shouldn't worry about what?" Jonas asked. His tone was light as he walked up to the table and placed the steaming cups down. "From Lily's expression, I think I must insist on knowing," he mused.

"I was just starting my own amazing conversation with Lily," Dani said. "But she was a bit worried about talking about you with me. I tried to explain it's perfectly fine. We're best friends and all."

Jonas grinned and shook his head. "I knew I shouldn't have left her with you."

"We're fine," I said, assuring him. "We spoke about balancing energy."

"Good." He winked at me, then turned to Dani, "So where is Paul tonight?"

"He told me he was studying for his recital, but I know he's on a group date," Dani said, laughing.

Jonas's jaw ticked. "So he's lying again."

Dani shrugged. "It's not that big of a deal. He's fifteen. We did worse."

Jonas smirked at her then grinned. "True. But I

won't let him get away with it."

"If you moved back from Texas," Dani said in a light tone.

Jonas's eyes dulled, but he said nothing more and sipped his chai. I reached under the table and touched his knee.

"My father used to go on tours," I offered, "but he always came through with a punishment when he got back." I laughed a little, and Dani and Alan joined in with me. Jonas's hand slipped under the table and squeezed mine.

"Don't get me wrong, Lily," Dani said, "I understand. But we all miss him here."

"We do," Alan chimed in support.

"I know. It won't be forever," Jonas said quietly. I squeezed his hand back.

"Oh, I got a call from Arthur about seeing you with a young lady this morning. He wanted to make sure I was okay," Dani said in a bored tone. "I told him."

"I told him too," Jonas said and exhaled. A bell sounded.

"The session starts in five minutes."

"We should get going," Alan announced. "Nice meeting you, Lily. We should do a dinner together." I shook his hand.

Dani gripped my face and kissed my cheeks. "Enjoy." Jonas tugged her arm and she giggled. "Don't worry, I didn't tell."

"I'll be right back." Jonas followed them out of the

café.

Dani Crane was a surprise. So easy and seeing their banter, though unfamiliar, relaxed me. She was so comfortable and welcoming to me. Not at all like I had imagined meeting an ex would be. Even Alan seemed awfully comfortable. My heart panged. They were like a family. A longing gripped me, but I took a deep breath and pushed my thoughts away. I didn't want to get caught up in the past.

Jonas returned with a bag in his hand, giving me one of his gorgeous smiles, "I apologize for that. Dani is just...."

My grin went lopsided. "—She's really just wow ... I don't know. I was nervous, but she was so kind."

Jonas smiled wistfully. "Dani is." He blew out. "My time in Texas has become a sore point for us. For Alan and Paul too. Thank you for that story about your father."

I shrugged. "It was true. He traveled at times, but we never felt he didn't care for us."

"I do care," Jonas said softly. "Anyway, I appreciated that." He tugged a little on my ponytail and I giggled for him. He took my hand and we walked up a flight of stairs and through a set of double doors. I stopped just inside, as my eyes took in the scenery.

The room, though dimly lit, was decorated as what I'd imagine to be an Arabian Tent. Beautiful colorful silk scarves draped along the ceiling, their soft edges brushing against the polished wood flooring. Like the rest of the center, the room had more floor pedestals with lit Eastern statues in the corners.

What captured my attention was the three makeshift tents in a triangle along the center of the room, complete with drop silks between them. The one at the top of the triangle was on a raised platform, lit with a large mattress in the center. There was a couple inside one tent. The other was unoccupied.

The doors closed and Padma and an elderly man, also wearing a tunic, walked past us and took a place in the middle, as Jonas led us over to the unoccupied tent.

"Namaste and welcome, everyone, to Tantra," Padma said. "Tonight's session goal is for couples and lovers to learn to communicate your sexual desires and embrace your sensuality."

My jaw unhinged. *He didn't.*

Jonas took my shoulder and leaned down next to my ear, "I thought you would enjoy this. Help you become more comfortable with your body and me."

I stared at him. I didn't know if I should be mad or happy that he had thought enough of me already to seek out a way to help us.

"This is Ravi," Padma said. She motioned to the elder man with short white hair dressed in loose pants standing next to her, love shining in her eyes. He kissed her palm before turning to the class.

"Thank you, Padma," Ravi said. "We will start with breathing and a little Hatha yoga to loosen you up. After every pose, we will return to the mountain pose."

Padma demonstrated by rolling her shoulders back and placing her palms together in front of her.

"You maintain contact with your partner," Ravi said. "We will give a question and you answer together. Let your mind rest and speak freely."

"After we loosen up, you may disrobe and get in your tent," Padma said. "Please set out your yoga mats so we can begin."

I trembled and Jonas hugged me closer. "I don't know if I can do this."

Jonas massaged my shoulders. "We'll go as far as you are comfortable." He unzipped his bag and pulled out mats.

"Face each other and maintain eye contact. Breathe in and exhale."

I stood in front of Jonas and felt a flutter through me. He was gorgeous.

"We start with the mountain pose," Ravi said. "We place our feet together then roll our shoulders back and put our palms together."

"Now for the first question. Say three things that come to mind when you think of sex," Padma said.

I tried to hold the pose and not giggle. "Naked. Exposed. Good."

"Touching. Feeling. Orgasm," Jonas said.

"Next pose. Inhale, extend your arms up, and place them flat on the floor ... exhale." Padma demonstrated and then we did the same pose.

"Breathe out and gaze at each other and ask your

partner, when you think of your body, what three words come to mind? Say it at the same time," Ravi said.

"Fit, athletic, healthy," he said with a smile on his lips.

"Curvy, fat, embarrassing," I said, then covered my mouth as Jonas frowned. He gave me a hug.

"Breathe in, and lunge with palms together over your head. Like this." Padma and Ravi demonstrated. "Now tell your partner three words that come to mind when you look at them. Same as before." We broke apart and I lunged with Jonas, then back to the mountain pose.

I grinned "Gorgeous, kind, demanding."

"Beautiful, sweet, sexy," Jonas said. We gazed at each other.

"Last poses, downward facing dog, into the cobra." Padma demonstrated by placing her hands flat on the mat and parting her legs, then lifting her hips in the air.

"Breathe," Padma said. She then moved her legs together behind her and dropped down, raising her upper body and lifting her chin in the air.

"Exhale. Back to the mountain pose. What three words come to mind when you think of having sex with your partner?"

"Aroused, excited, enjoyment," he said.

I smiled. "Nervous, aroused, excited."

Jonas took my hand. "Relax. I want you to enjoy this." He led me to the tent and we climbed inside. He pulled his shirt over his head, revealing his ripped upper body.

I trembled and looked around, only to find the others engrossed in their partners.

"Eyes on me," Jonas said, calling me back to him. He pulled off his pants, no underwear. His cock was exposed and jutting out from his body before me. He was like a sculpted work of art, utter perfection. Waves of heat flowed through me as my pulse pounded in my chest. I was spellbound, my eyes not able to stray from him.

He knelt before me and touched my knees. "You want me to take them off you?" Jonas asked in a low tone.

Could I do this? I blinked and nodded. He reached for my shirt and tugged it off, leaving my upper body naked. I automatically reached up and shielded my breasts, though my mind was quick to remind me that he had seen and touched more just last night.

He reached for my waist and worked my pants and panties together down my legs, placing them to the side with his clothing. He took in a sharp breath, his eyes looking over me approvingly, and the tension I didn't realize I was holding eased.

"We won't have sex here. This is just part of the practice," he said.

"Now I want you to get in the yab-yum," Padma called out.

I turned my head and gazed over their naked forms as Ravi stood immodestly naked, then sat down and crossed his legs. Padma straddled his lap and wrapped her legs around his torso, settling her hands on his shoulders. Ravi moved closer, pressing himself up against her, neither breaking eye contact.

"Gaze at each other. See the goddess and god within each other. See the desire your lover has for you," Padma said.

My eyes widened as I turned to Jonas and he expertly took the seated posture. He reached for me and I settled myself in his lap, wrapping my legs around his lower back. He pulled me close, pressing my sex up against his. I looked up into his face and felt energy course through my body, taking my breath away.

"Inhale and exhale. Use your senses. See, smell, and feel each other."

Jonas's eyes never strayed from mine. I could see his desire there, but a warmth was there as well, that made a lump form in my throat as my pulse pounded in my chest. This close, I felt his heart pumping as hard as mine. The twitch of his cock against me made wetness gush between my thighs. My eyes dilated and I felt as if my whole body was swelling with desire for him. I inhaled and could smell his aftershave and my perfume mixing together, along with our sexual scent.

"Jonas," I whispered. He rubbed my back soothingly. The need for him was overwhelming me. Inadvertently, I started rocking my pelvis against him. Jonas fought to maintain his pose, but I could see in his eyes the effect my movement had on him.

We continued to stare deeply at each other, nothing about us able to hide. It was raw and intimate, and the jolting of our connection seemed almost tangible. He wanted me, just as much as I wanted him. My body quivered as I pressed harder against his erection. We breathed together, heavily and in sync. I was burning and I could feel my sex throbbing against his, the ache building more until it was all I could think of.

"Now, move your hands over each other," Ravi said.

I shook my head. *I can't last another minute in this class.* I felt like I was sinking. I pleaded as much as I could through my eyes. "I need you now. Can we please go?"

Jonas paused and studied me, then mercifully lifted me off his lap. "I'll take you back now."

I crawled away from him and quickly put on my shirt and pants, then waited impatiently as Jonas put on his. We eased out of the tent and Jonas quickly collected his bag. From the noises in the other tent, I gathered the other couple couldn't wait either. Jonas, as quietly as possible, eased open the door and we left the room.

We moved back to the alcove and put on our shoes. Jonas pulled me hard against him and kissed me deeply. Wrapping myself around him like a pole, I couldn't get close enough. If he wanted to take me that minute, I would have let him.

"I've got you." Jonas lifted me up and carried me out of the house. Once we were outside, he put me down and gave me one of his incredible smiles, which I reflected back to him.

I said a brief hello to David and we entered the car.

Once the doors were closed, Jonas reached for me and lifted my shirt up and over my head. I didn't protest. I didn't want to wait to reach the hotel, and apparently neither did he. He gripped my swollen breasts, kissing and sucking them. I arched into him, my hands gripping his hair. I leaned down for more kisses, which Jonas gave to me, covering my lips before sweeping in with his tongue. I moaned against his mouth as I tugged at his shirt and he pulled it over his head.

Raking my fingers over his chest, I shifted on his lap, onto his hard erection. Jonas groaned, and when he reached for my pants I just kicked off my shoes. He didn't stop, but pulled the fabric down my legs. I reached for his pants impatiently, as Jonas brushed his fingers against my throbbing sex. "Please, Jonas."

"I've got you, Lily." He pulled me in his lap and pressed his cock at my entrance, gripping my hips and lowering me down on him until he was seated deep inside me. I cried out at the sensation of him stretching and filling me.

Moaning, he moved me up and down on his cock.

"Oh, Jonas." I leaned in and kissed over his face and grabbed his hair.

He grunted as he bit down on my neck, thrusting up, harder and faster inside me. He reached his hand between us and pressed and stroked my clit. I cried out loudly, clamping down on his cock in climax.

"Lily, so good. I...." He became incoherent as he struggled to keep going as my inner walls squeezed his cock. Sliding me down on the seat, he thrust in harder and faster, until he released hotly inside me.

Jonas didn't stop there, but rolled his hips and stroked again as I spasmed around him still riding my climax as another erupted in me. I bit my lip hard, then gave in to my cry as Jonas growled out. He held onto me, kissing my forehead and my lips as we both worked to catch our breath. When we eased, he lifted off of me.

He reached for his pants. "I'm…." He didn't finish, and I felt the same way. The sex blew my mind. The connection, and the orgasm, was more than I had ever experienced before. Did he feel it too?

My eyes felt heavy as I wobbled to get my clothing.

"I'll help." Jonas reached into a compartment and took out some cloths, then lifted my legs open and started cleaning me.

I could only manage to pant. I was aroused, but also drained. *Doesn't he have any idea what that's doing to me?* "This was too intimate, Jonas. I don't think you should do that."

"What?" Jonas asked, giving me a lascivious grin. "Make you come or wipe my cum from your pussy?"

Reaching for my pants and shirt, his crass response had my skin burning and had me thinking he had purposely been that way to throw off my response to his actions. But I decidedly opened up and told him exactly what I was thinking, "The second. It's too intimate. It sort of confuses me. This evening was for couples…."

He paused this time, as if he was contemplating what

I had said to him. After a minute or so, he spoke, "The Tantra was to make you comfortable in our companionship. I travel and won't be here all the time. This was a jumpstart charge for us if you may, on being comfortable with each other."

I licked my lips. I couldn't explain it to him. It was something about the way he looked at me. It had desire and amusement all mixed together. It made me feel silly and sexy at the same time. He was right. I did feel less self-conscious and more comfortable with him. So it was a way to bring on our sexual intimacy. "Oh. Okay. I guess."

"You guess?" Jonas mused. "Come here." He kissed the side of my face and put his arm around me. I knew his holding me had nothing to do with sexual intimacy, but I hid my face against him and sunk into the warmth of his arms, inhaling his incredible scent. Seeing, feeling, touching, and cultivating our companionship as we rode back to the hotel for the rest of the evening.

CHAPTER ELEVEN

I COULDN'T LOOK David in the eye as we climbed out of the car. I knew my appearance must have matched up with what he undoubtedly heard. My clothing was wrinkled and my ponytail lopsided, with some of my hair escaping it. Not to mention my swollen lips and glazed stare. I looked like just what I had been up to, fucking in the back of a car.

Moving through the lobby of the hotel, I looked over Jonas as he strolled next to me. He was slightly tousled, in his shirt and loose pants, and from the gawking hotel guests, exceedingly handsome. As if he hadn't just shared the same experience as me at all.

"You alright, Lily?" Jonas asked, interrupting my thoughts as we climbed in the elevator.

I nodded, but didn't turn my head. I could feel his stare as we rode up to the suite.

I was alright, wasn't I?

I climbed out and followed him to the door, walking in and quietly putting my things away as he took out his phone and started back to business.

I stood there for a minute, rubbing the center of my chest.

"Lily?" A slight rise to his voice. "Are you listening? I asked what you would like for dinner."

I looked over at him and suddenly burst into tears. I had no idea why I was crying, but Jonas dropped his call and crossed the room, enveloping me. Pressing my head against his chest, tears continued to fall.

"Shhh. It'll be alright," he whispered.

I didn't know why he said that to me, but it resulted in me leaning into the comfort he was readily willing to give. He walked us to the couch and surprised me by pulling me onto his lap.

Was it the Tantra?

All I knew was that the connection had me wanting him in ways I knew I shouldn't. Comforting wasn't part of the companionship, was it? Maybe he was right. I was too inexperienced to handle this. But the thought of backing out made me sob all the more, I didn't want to not see Jonas. As I continued to cry, he whispered soothing words and stroked my back. When I had no more tears left, I stilled.

"Look at me." Jonas captured my chin and I looked at him as tears started leaking out my eyes again. "Tell me what you are feeling."

I gulped in air. I couldn't tell him that the intimacy was already making me want a relationship. How could this be? We had only just met and started spending time together. Still, I felt closer to him in a way I never experienced with Declan. Sure, in our three years together I loved and learned a lot about him; however, I rarely recall him ever asking about my life or how I was feeling. Sex was our intimacy, but that's where it ended. I was the one he leaned on to pick him up when he was down. When my parents were gone and I found I needed to be picked up, he wasn't there or willing to give it to me. When he broke up with me and left, he took himself, his friends, and his life with him.

My heart felt heavy with the weight of my loneliness. No calls, no comfort, or care. And here I was now with a man I barely knew that went out of his way to try to make a connection with me. Touched me intimately and didn't end it there when he could. He was right before me, still asking and wanting to know about me. I looked up at him and the warmth and concern reflected in his eyes made my chest ache. *This is wrong*, I thought. I needed to distance myself from him and keep what we had working for the both of us. I decided to tell him what I could, and what I hoped he would accept.

"The Tantra was intense. I just need a shower and some sleep. I didn't know it would feel like that. And then … the car." My breath hitched.

Jonas exhaled long. "Tantra is intense. Maybe it was too much too fast." He studied me and I fought not to avert my eyes.

I plastered on a smile. I was falling for him and I knew that it was too fast. "I just need a shower and some sleep," I repeated to him.

He leaned down and kissed me tenderly. "You haven't had dinner."

I shook my head, "I'm not hungry. Just tired…."

"Because you didn't eat anything," Jonas said, irritation in his tone. "I wasn't happy with what you said about your body during the workshop, either. Is that why you try to avoid eating?"

I chewed my lip. "I just want to be healthy."

"Part of being healthy is taking care of yourself," he said. "As my companion, I expect you to eat with me."

I tried to muster a frown in protest, but I felt drained. Perhaps he was right. *Maybe I'm hungry.* I tried to recall what I had eaten during the day, but couldn't. I nodded to him.

"Good. What would you like for dinner?" Jonas asked. He moved me next to him and grabbed a menu.

"Soup and a salad," I said, hunching my shoulders.

"Red snapper and chocolate ice cream for dessert," Jonas said and winked at me.

My jaw dropped. "Why did you ask what I wanted?" I asked when he hung up the phone.

"I won't next time," Jonas said bluntly.

I smirked and then laughed, suddenly feeling slightly better. "You're bossy. Luckily, I like red snapper and chocolate ice cream."

He chuckled then pulled me close, nuzzling my neck. "I enjoyed tonight, but I barely got a taste of you. I want more."

I clung to him then, burying my face in his neck and

inhaling. "I want more, too."

"Soon. I'll just need to check on a few things. Go have your shower, and I'll have mine."

I dutifully stood up, and Jonas went back to his work at his desk. I sighed and went into the bathroom. Turning on the shower and climbing in, I scrubbed over myself with a lavender wash. When I was finished, I dried myself, only to realize I didn't have any clothing in the room.

"Just put on the robe," Jonas said from behind me. "Saves me the time of taking it off you after dinner."

I dipped my head and grinned as my pulse sped up.

"Lovely." His gaze lazing over me approvingly. He kissed me lightly on the lips. "Dinner is here. I'll be out soon. You can pour our drinks and turn on music if you like."

I slipped on the robe and cinched it, then turned to watch Jonas turn on the shower, and strip out of his clothing. I stood for a moment, admiring his muscular physique and the fact that he was comfortable with himself and his body.

"You keep staring, I'm going to pull you in here," Jonas said in a baritone. I didn't move and he laughed. "Go on."

I reluctantly walked out of the bathroom and over to the dining table where I poured a Scotch neat for him and a glass of white wine for me. I next walked over and turned on the radio, surprised to find an easy listening station. *When did he listen to this?* I giggled. Walking a couple of steps to the window, I parted it and glanced down, and saw the constant stream of traffic. So many cars, and people. *I'm just a drop in this metropolis.*

The sound of the door opening alerted me to Jonas walking out in one of the white terry cloth robes that unfortunately reached his knees. Still, his tanned and toned muscular legs were eye feasts—as well as a peek of his groomed chest hair. He strolled over towards the stereo.

"What? It's relaxing," he muttered and I laughed.

He then walked over to the dining table and pulled out my seat. *Ever the gentleman.* I walked over and sat down, lifting my face to the kiss he had waiting for me. He uncovered our meals, then joined me. My mouth watered at the sight of the grilled red snapper, yellow tomato sulis, and sautéed green beans. I looked over at Jonas's grilled lobster and vegetable salad.

"May I make the quote for tonight?" I asked.

He smiled and nodded. So I raised my glass and said, "From Byron: Be thou the rainbow in storms of life. The evening beams that smiles the clouds away, and tints tomorrow with prophetic rays. May our smiles shared henceforth, brighten this evening and beyond."

Jonas practically beamed at me. "You constantly surprise me," Jonas said and raised his glass to me. After a few minutes of eating, Jonas asked, "So, where are we in our conversation?"

I took a sip of my wine. "I'm not sure. We talked about family, and I met Alan and Dani tonight."

"Yes. You did," he said. "Alan is a corporate lawyer, well he was mine."

I reached for his hand and he patted mine.

"I'm not upset about them being together. Alan is a good man, and he always puts his personal life first. He's what she needs," Jonas said. "We've been more friends for the past few years than lovers anyway." He shook his head. "I don't know why I say these things to you."

I took his hand. "Maybe because I'm a good listener and I won't judge you."

He eyed me speculatively and then nodded. "Yes. I believe that's part of it.'

We ate a few minutes in silence. "With Declan, we weren't friends. We were basically opposites. But I think we both just wanted to be in a relationship. We didn't want to be alone. I knew I didn't, especially after my parents died."

"If you don't mind me asking, why did you stay?" Jonas asked.

My looked down at my plate. "I didn't want to give up. I wanted to become whatever he needed me to be. I thought if I worked hard at it … Hell, I would still be working, if he hadn't broken it off with me."

"I guess that's another thing we have in common," he said wistfully. "I tried to have it all, but never found a balance. I knew we weren't working anymore, but I stayed for Paul. It took Dani moving on with Alan for me to let go."

We gazed at each other for a moment, and I thought

about the Tantra, tuning into your lovers feelings. I knew in that moment we were synced.

Jonas turned and picked up his Scotch. "Listen to us. This is supposed to be a light dinner."

I snorted. "We can leave it in our conversation." I leaned over as he placed his lips on mine, capturing my mouth in a slow coaxing kiss, which he made deeper as his tongue moved in and tangled with mine, coiling the muscles low on my body. I moaned against his lips, running my hands underneath his robe and over his hard upper body and smooth chest hair.

"Soon," Jonas said, easing my hand away.

I whimpered and he grinned at me. We went back to eating our meal. I knew the red snapper was delicious, but my mind had wandered off to the sexual promise Jonas had made to me. He had awakened that need in me and I was ready for him to take me again.

"What are you doing?" Jonas asked, interrupting my thoughts.

I startled and looked at him, only to find his eyes were gazing down my body.

I had inadvertently moved my chair back and opened my robe. My face heated as I moved to cinch it back in place.

"Don't," he said. "You need me."

I started to protest, but he interrupted me by saying, "I need you too. There is no shame in needing sex. No shame in seeking it with me."

My lips parted and my body ignited as his eyes roved

over my exposed skin. "I need you," I repeated his words.

"Take off your robe," Jonas commanded.

My hands shook as I gaped it open.

He moved out of the seat and dropped to his knees before me.

"If you want me there, open your legs wider." I did as he instructed, moving them as wide as the chair. He lifted one of my legs on his shoulder and stared, then met my eyes.

"You're drenched. Your clit is swollen." He touched my hot, soaked pussy with his fingers and moaned. Dragging his tongue through my slick folds, then sucked my clit in his mouth.

I moaned and gripped the chair, feeling the impending climax already. "Oh, Jonas. I'm going to come."

He pushed two fingers inside me as he teased my clit, and I ground myself against him and cried out his name as I came.

Jonas wasn't done. He pulled me off the chair and lowered my head to his cock.

"Suck." I did, suppressing a gag as he pushed himself to the back of my throat with a groan.

"Oh, Lily." I gripped his tight ass, and greedily slid my tongue around his shaft and sucked, then bobbed up and down on his cock. He grabbed my hair and tugged it, easing his cock out of my mouth. He leaned down and took my distended clit, drawing deeply on it, causing me to cry out incoherently.

"Mmm. Do that again." He pushed in with his fingers and I arched and cried out once more, so close to orgasm again.

He moved up and guided his cock to my entrance. "Not yet. Come on my cock." In an instant, he picked me up and carried me. His hunger and need was rawer for me this time, and he didn't waste another minute before taking me. I gripped his neck hard and opened my legs wide as he lifted me onto his thick, long length and pushed himself in until he shielded himself deep inside me. I cried out in pleasure and pain.

Jonas didn't stop, but pulled back and rolled his hips against me. "Lily." My back met the wall and I dug my heels into him as he started to relentlessly pound inside me.

"Come," he gritted as he slammed and moved against me. I moved and panted hard, my inner walls constricting and my orgasm bursting free over me. I quivered and spasmed as he let go and came hot inside me. My walls gripped him tight, milking all he had to give to me. We both fought to recover as we kissed feverishly across each other's faces. Our eyes met and a sizzle burned between us.

My pulse pounded in my ears as emotions started welling inside my chest. Did he feel it too? He closed his eyes and kissed me sweetly on the lips. He eased me to the floor and I wobbled as I tried to gain my footing. My face pressed against the sweat on his chest, his heart pounding hard as we both worked to catch our breaths. He lifted me up without a word and carried me to his bed where we rested, then started all over again.

CHAPTER TWELVE

I have a press conference at the Clift Hotel and a work dinner tonight.

I sighed as I looked down at my phone and read Jonas's text.

Okay. Should I go back to the hotel?
I'd like you to meet me there at the atrium.

I looked at the time, 3:48 p.m. *On 44th? Okay. What time?* I replied.

6:00 p.m. Good. Look forward to seeing you.

"See you soon," I repeated as I placed the phone down. A flutter went through my chest as I contemplated the "looking forward to seeing you" part of his message. Was it an endearment? He was leaving in two days and I couldn't shake him from my thoughts, or the grin from my face. The last two nights had been like a dream come true. He was not only an incredible lover, but attentive. He went out of his way to make things happen and was considerate, calling to invite me to a work dinner. But what I found hard to dismiss was the way he made a fuss over me. Just like Declan had been in the beginning, he used to practically baby me. I stared off at nothing, allowing my mind to drift off into a memory of the early years in our relationship.

"You are so beautiful to me," Declan sang. "Did you know you're the most beautiful girl here?"

I giggled. "Oh, Dec," I sighed, smoothing my hands over his tuxedo as we danced together at his best friend Callum's wedding reception. I liked seeing Declan outside of the jeans and shirts he wore every day.

Declan said, "No one holds a candle to you here. So thin." His large hands clasped my waist. "Well, you were," he teased.

I rolled my eyes as I glanced down at my silvery gray baby doll dress. A little snug at the waist. "I thought you said it was a sign of happiness."

He held on to me and kissed up my neck. "I'm just messing." He kissed my lips. "You'll need that extra weight when we start our family."

My eyes widened. "You asking me to marry you?" I blurted out.

He squinted. "Soon. When I know I can provide a good life for us."

I nodded and looked away. Two years. My heart heavy. "I don't care."

He shook his head. "Nope. Your father does. And I'll show him just how wrong he is about me."

I averted my eyes. "My father likes you. He doesn't talk bad about you." Not really all bad.

He kissed my lips again. "I don't care if he does. He's

*not in control anymore, and it bothers him. I can under-
stand that. He loves you. You were his little girl, now you're
mine."*

*My chest warmed and I beamed at him. "Oh Dec. I...."
I looked down.*

*"I love you, Princess," Declan said. "I know I don't say
it, but I do. I always have."*

*I threw my hands around his neck. He loves me! "I love
you too, Dec."*

My chest throbbed as the memory lingered over me.
Callum had only just met his girl and they were married
in less than a year. Two years to finally hear "I love you"
back. *Never again will I waste my time pinning for those
words to be said back to me.* My mood had soured as I
leaned on my elbow and turned my attention to the
announcements Gregor had sent me to work on. I threw
myself into my tasks to distract the dark places my mind
was headed.

At five-thirty, I pressed the busy button on my phone
and grabbed my handbag off my desk, then headed
straight to the bathroom. Standing before the row of
sinks, I rinsed my mouth with mouthwash, removed the
chignon from my hair and fluffed out the waves. I wasn't
sure which way Jonas liked it. I groaned. *Silly me. Already
thinking about pleasing a man that was more of a new
friend than lover. No good getting hung up on a man that
doesn't want a commitment.* My heart panged as I scolded
myself. Sighing, I adjusted my grey pencil skirt, making
sure there were no runs in my nylons. My phone beeped

and I took it out, looking down at the message.

Take off your panties before you arrive.

My body heated as waves of desire coursed through me. Did I want to play his game? I looked down at my pencil skirt. It reached just above my knees and I would be wearing my winter coat. Only the two of us would know. *So why not?* I thought mischievously. I slipped in a stall and quickly removed my panties, tucking them in my handbag. As I smoothed my skirt back in place, I instantly felt too naked. Still, my mind and body were focused on sex and the next few nights, just as I believed Jonas wanted me to be. *Easy.* How easy he had me still made me uncomfortable. I didn't even last a day before I was naked in his bed. And the thought of what he did to me inflamed me. Shamefully, I couldn't wait for it to happen again. After following his explicit orders, I was practically desperate for it.

After freshening my lip gloss, I walked out of the bathroom and put on my coat, then headed down the stairs to the lobby.

Once there, I walked outside and gasped as a bite of wind caught my breath. The sky was heavily clouded and reminded me of Quincy right before a new snowfall. I clasped the top of my coat tighter around my neck and joined the other office drones grouping down the sidewalk of East 44th. Busy. Suits, the homeless, and tourists looking up at the skyscrapers all made navigation difficult, but I managed to zig my way across Bryan Park to the Clift Hotel. The adrenaline buzzed through me as

I made my way inside, the modern chic mahogany wood and pastel furnishings were appealing, signs for the conference posted throughout the hotel garnered my attention. There was one outside the Velvet Room lounge that displayed, *Generation Y Business and Beyond*, with equally large billing being given to the star guest speaker, *Jonas Crane*. There was a standing room only press event taking place. I eased my way through the crowd and found a spot along the wall that fortunately provided the least obstructed view of the front of the room.

As I settled in my spot, my ears singled out a familiar baritone voice coming over the microphone. My gaze shifted to the front of the room and the man seated at the center of the large table dressed in a white shirt and eloquently cut gray suit. *Jonas.* The sight of him stole my breath away and quickened my already racing pulse. He was the epitome of physical perfection. I was mesmerized, staring in awe of him.

When I managed to tear my gaze away, I noticed I wasn't alone. Everyone in the room was spellbound by his presence, hanging on his every word. Even the reporters were charmed, filtering all their questions to him. With the rapid flickering of the flashing cameras, I'd imagine being under the spotlight was too much. But no one would have guessed from the way Jonas handled himself. He was effortless, not a tremor or hesitation. He was in his element. Standing there, I was amazed at his self-confidence. I wondered what it would feel like to have a fraction of what he seemed to have in abundance.

The thunderous applause woke me from my melancholy, and the present pressed upon me as the room started to clear out. I edged closer towards the front. The closer I came, the more dynamic Jonas seemed, until I felt as if I was an ant before a mountain.

His gaze peered out and connected with mine. A jolt of electricity went through me, flaring our contact, our connection. He started to move with purpose away from his business harem and over towards me, like a predator ready to strike. My heart thumped hard within my chest the closer he came, until a staccato filled my ears. I remained frozen to the spot like prey, my eyes wide and ready to be taken. And I had no doubt he would take me. Once I stood before him, his hands rose, cupping my face and tilting me up to him. His piercing eyes connected with mine, and my heart pounded against my ribcage, as his gaze penetrated me.

"You're tense?" Jonas smiled.

My cheeks warmed as I tried to form words under his intense gaze. "Yes. A little, I suppose."

"We're having dinner at Koi Restaurant with a friend of mine tonight. Wish I could take you back to the Astoria right now, but I need this meeting before I leave town," he said.

I half-lidded my eyes. "It's fine."

"It will be." He clasped my hand and walked us to the front of the hall. My brows lifted. "Koi's in the other direction, Jonas…." He didn't answer, just walked us around the panel table and behind the curtain. He stopped us in a small, dimly lit hallway near an exit. He placed my coat on top of his briefcase, then held his arms out wide.

"Come here, beautiful," Jonas purred. He gripped my hips hard, then captured my mouth in a kiss. He immediately deepened it as his tongue licked along mine, filling it with a fresh taste of mint. I met his kiss with my own demanding, feverish strokes of my tongue as I melted against him. When we broke away, we were both breathing heavily.

The front of my body was pressed against his erection, which was growing heavy against me. I moaned and withered against him as my body was awakened to his touch, wanting more.

I rubbed my legs together. "This isn't making me relax." I looked around. "It's not private either. Is there somewhere else we can go?"

His eyelids hooded. "I prefer here." He pressed his body in again.

I puffed out. "Someone could come back here."

Jonas didn't answer, just moved his hand to the back of my thigh, lifting my skirt as he eased the fabric upward. Goose bumps broke across my naked flesh, and I panted as his hand stroked the skin on my buttocks. He moved his hand up and pressed my head against his chest while the other worked around the front to grip my mound.

"Mmm ... you don't feel like you want to wait," Jonas said darkly. His fingers stroked, pushing inside me.

I inhaled sharply and his scent intoxicated me. Jonas had me. The knowledge that he could place me in a compromising position so near a room still occupied by people should have infuriated me. But I couldn't think as my body gave into the pleasure he was giving me.

I whimpered in frustration as I parted my thighs and moved against his hand, allowing him to rob me of my sanity. "Please," I spluttered.

"Yes," Jonas said, in triumph as his fingers stroked true against my slick sex. He had my surrender. His pace increased, making me moan and move against him. I could feel the pressure building.

"Come," he growled, he pinched my clit and I came withering under his grasp as he held me. Closing my eyes I leaned my head into his chest.

His demeanor was calm, but his heart pounded just as hard as mine. When I stilled, he inhaled against my hair and slowly released me.

I glanced at him through my lashes as I pulled my skirt down. I felt like I had been working out for hours, and was ready to crash. "We could have gotten caught. Your reputation would have been ruined," I griped.

Jonas shrugged as he wiped his hands on his handkerchief. "Security is around. No one would have been allowed to follow me."

I gasped, "So you planned this?"

He kissed me. "I plan everything."

I looked away. *He planned.* Was I that predictable, or

did all the women from his past so easily give in to his wishes? I had little doubt of that. But he was just as turned on as I was, and I realized I was being selfish too. "What about you?"

He smiled warmly at me. "You can ask me again when we get back." He kissed me lightly on the lips and led me to a restroom, where we both had a chance to right ourselves.

When we came out, he pressed his hand on my back and led us toward the entrance of the Koi restaurant in the hotel. Standing by the door was a good-looking blonde male in similar business attire as Jonas. His eyes were a deep blue, his gaze pointed as he approached us.

"Lily, this is Ian Unger," Jonas explained, a curve on his lips. "My lawyer and friend," he added lightly.

Ian took my hand and grasped it firmly. His eyes flicked over me from head to toe as his full lips spread into a wide grin. "Very nice to meet you, Lily."

Jonas tucked me against his side and moved us through the door that Ian held open. I couldn't help but cover my grin at his impulse to stake a claim on me. Did he not see all the people at the conference, and now the restaurant, craning their necks for a glimpse of him? I had more of a reason to try to mark him, even though I knew I couldn't. Still, I marveled at this beautiful powerful man and his possessiveness of me.

We grouped through the doors and up to the dining area. Jonas barely made it inside before people came up to speak with him. He somehow had the skill to move through them, while keeping me tucked to his side.

The glitzy décor was modern Asian, dark bamboo with a gorgeous lattice honeycomb art piece. Koi was one of the chic eateries, which would have normally put me on edge. But the softly lit ambiance, along with the after work crowd, gave off a relaxing vibe that I held onto as we moved towards the hostess podium for a table. We didn't have to wait, as on approach the hostess walked around her podium and led us down toward a private booth, away from the rows of leather plush tables. Jonas helped me into my seat in the far corner of our booth and sat down next to me, whilst Ian positioned himself across from us.

"Ian is the reason I have been in Texas so long," Jonas said. "He has been taking his time on the acquisition of Klein Technologies."

Ian chuckled. "Oh no, you can't blame that on me. I'm taking my Tribeca home back in a few weeks. You're the one still holding up there."

"Because it's not solid," Jonas said dryly. "And you should be there."

Ian smirked at Jonas. "Let's not bore Lily with business."

I glanced at Jonas. "I don't mind. Thanks."

He turned and grinned at me. "Lily is too sweet and polite to say otherwise. But I agree. Let's not talk about work." He winked at me.

A waitress came over and took our drink orders, announcing the dinner specials.

"Sake for Lily, and a Scotch for me. Sushi Matsu, Sashimi take…." Jonas said, along with a few other orders. Way more than I would ever eat. I reached under the table and tugged his hand as the waitress turned to Ian.

My brow lowered. "Hey. What was that? I don't even know half of what you ordered," I whispered.

"You mind? I thought it would be fun to try a few things," Jonas mused.

"I do, too. But you didn't even ask," I whispered.

"Because you would have ordered a salad, and that's not enough for a woman that had only a yogurt or cereal this morning." He leaned over and pressed his lips to the side of my face.

I shuttered my eyes and tried to suppress my grin. When I leaned back, I noticed Ian staring at me. He cleared his throat.

"Make that another Scotch," Ian said. The waitress beamed at the two men, mouthed "wow" to me, and smiled back agreeably. She returned a few seconds later with a small assortment of bread, cheese, and olives.

"Have you ever been to San Francisco, Lily?" Ian asked. "I'm trying to talk Jonas into coming to a conference there."

"No," I said, taking a sip of my drink and sucking in. Strong. "From what I can see, it's beautiful. I always wanted to visit."

"Yes. It's one of my favorite cities," Ian said. "Not that I will get to see much of it when we go there."

"Muir Woods is the place I always wanted to see," I said. "Well, the forest moon of Endor," I muttered.

Jonas eyed me inquisitively, while Ian laughed, "You're a Star Wars fan?"

I blushed. "Yeah. A bit."

"She has a shrine to them in her bedroom," Jonas said teasingly.

Jonas reached out his hand and tucked my hair behind my ear.

Ian stared back at him and took a sip of his Scotch. "So. What would you like to discuss with Burt?" he asked, and they launched into a business discussion.

So much for not talking about it, I thought. The waitress returned with a large platter of sushi. Jonas moved his hand to my thigh. I gasped, and I tried to cover it with a cough. I could see a little smile play on his lips as he continued to speak to Ian.

Jonas's phone went off. When he answered it, his face lit up. "Paul. Yes. You're all set." Jonas moved it away from his mouth and turned to me, "I'll be right back." He stood and walked away from the table.

I stared after him. His delight and eagerness to speak to his son I found touching. I wondered dreamily if he ever had that look on his face for me. My stomach warmed as admiration for him filled me once again. He must have felt it because he immediately looked back at me.

"Lily," Ian said, calling my attention to him.

I turned my head to him and his lips parted.

"So, I hear you met at Sir Harry's? You're a publishing assistant?" Ian asked.

I laughed and nodded. "Yes. I work at Arch Limited. I tried to contact him about his book," I said and sipped my drink.

"For the book," Ian said and lifted the corner of his mouth. "I want to read it too, but he's been quite tight lipped about it. You know if you ever do go out to San Francisco, I know a few people there. I actually toured Skywalker ranch."

A grin spread across my face and I mockingly clasped my chest. "Oh my God. Wow. Did you take photos?"

Ian's smile broadened. "Of course I did." We laughed. "Now I'm smiling. Your smile is infectious," he said quietly.

Jonas came back to the table and I turned to him.

"Paul was trying to squeeze in a few friends with him for his visit with me," Jonas said, the corners of his mouth turned up.

"He doesn't want to hang out with his dad. Give him a break," Ian said. "You didn't give in?"

"Nope," Jonas said, lifting his chin and taking a sip of his drink. "I did, however, agree that he can meet a friend already living here."

I ate a few bites and put my fork down.

"A little more, Lily," Jonas said softly. He held out his chopsticks with a beefy slice of salmon before my lips.

I lidded my eyes. "I'm full."

Jonas leaned next to my ear and said. "You'll need

your strength."

"Jonas," I said in mock annoyance.

His lips twitched.

"That's sweet," Ian said and chuckled.

Jonas didn't say anything, but continued to feed me more until I placed my hand over my mouth in mock refusal, which made Ian laugh all the more.

"Lily, if you ever want to see those photos of my trip to Skywalker ranch...." Ian said. He reached in his coat and handed me a card.

Jonas looked at Ian. "What photos?" his tone light.

I smiled. "Ian is a Star Wars fan, and he said he has pictures of a tour of the Skywalker ranch."

Jonas's eyes flashed at Ian. "Oh, did he?"

"Yes." Ian cleared his throat. "I visited a while ago. Since I'm here now, I thought I could show her the photos if she wanted to see them. As a fellow fan."

Jonas merely stared at him.

I reached under the table and squeezed Jonas's hand. "I'm fine. I don't need to see. Thank you."

"No," Jonas said. "Maybe we can all do this together sometime."

I broadened my smile and let go of the breath I hadn't even known I was holding. "Yeah. I'd like that."

"Sounds like a plan," Ian said evenly. "So, Jonas, do you think we can reach Steven...?" He launched into a renewed conversation about business.

I sipped a little of the sake and listened as Jonas spoke, his inflection and tone so confident. I marveled at his ability to negotiate. Hell, whatever he said he had sold me, though I wondered why he invited me to dine with them in the first place. Finally, he motioned for the waitress to come and paid the bill. Then we all walked out of the restaurant, Ian stopping at the door. "This is where I leave you two." He tilted his head. "Very nice to meet you, Lily. Jonas, I'll see you soon."

As we moved to the car, I couldn't help but feel a distance from Jonas. I wondered if I had done something wrong, though Jonas hadn't said anything. When we settled in the car, I glanced over at him. "Is everything alright?" He pulled me close to his side and kissed my lips. "Everything is fine. Just Ian testing me."

"Testing you in what way?" I asked as David pulled right into gridlock traffic.

Jonas exhaled. "Trying to," he paused, "never mind." He kissed my lips lightly.

Once the door was closed, I smiled and scooted a little closer to him.

"I know you like Star Wars, but…." Jonas said.

"But you don't want me hanging out with Ian while you're out of town," I said, peering at him through my lashes.

"That obvious, I suppose," Jonas said, looking straight ahead. "It's not that I don't trust you. I don't trust him. Don't get me wrong, Ian is probably as close to a friend outside of Dani that I have." He turned his head and looked at me. "But we are just getting … used to each other. I would rather we spend time together."

Jonas, insecure? I stared at him in bewilderment. "Ian seems nice and all, but I don't feel the same way I feel about…." I let the words die as I held my own uncertainties. Jonas reached out and placed his arm around me. I sunk in against him as we rode through the night traffic.

The sounds of the sirens, and beeping horns blocked out the quiet that settled between us. The thoughts of having Jonas still ruled my mind as we made our way over to Park Avenue and back to the Astoria. Once out of the car, Jonas kept me close as we made our way back up to his suite. However, when we reached the suite, I felt a shift between us.

"Remove your clothes," Jonas commanded the second the door was closed.

My lips parted. "Right now? Come on. Can't you just take me?" I said, laughing as I removed my coat and hung it in the closet.

"Is that your fantasy?" Jonas asked with a salacious grin. "If you want to try a capture fantasy, I'd be open to hearing about it. And any others you have."

I flushed. "Maybe. I don't know. I just feel under the spotlight undressing for you."

"I like you under my spotlight," Jonas said, his gaze heavy on me.

A tingle went through me and my pulse increased. "Do you have a fantasy?"

"Yes," Jonas paused as if relishing my apt attention, "that's the look of my fantasies. Your attention and eagerness to please me."

I sucked my bottom lip in. I couldn't deny it. "That's the part that gets me in trouble."

"Not with me," Jonas said. "My fantasy has you naked at my feet, ready and eager to do anything and everything I ask of you."

I covered my face to hide my reaction. *That sounds hot, except for the naked part.*

Jonas walked over and tugged my hands down. "You like that part. It gets better." He pecked my lips. "But you're not ready for that." He removed his shoes and suit jacket, then walked further into the room. I followed after him, until he stopped inside the bedroom and hung the jacket inside a closet there, then sat down on the king-sized bed.

He held out his hand. "Follow me."

My nipples hardened as heat sparked inside me. I took his hand.

"That's the look I enjoy seeing on you," he said.

My mouth went dry as I pulled the end of my dress up and over my head, revealing my white lace bra.

"I'm speechless, Lily," his response was husky and deep. "You make it hard to show any restraint around you."

My hands shook as I eased my bra down my arms and off. His breathing quickened as he watched me bend down and fold my clothes for him.

I stood and handed him the pile. Placing them on the side table, Jonas sat back and adjusted the front of his pants. My breathing grew ragged as his gaze roamed over me.

Jonas stood up. "Lay down on your back and spread your legs."

Pulling back the duvet and climbing on the bed, I trembled in anticipation as I spread my legs. His gaze was on my pussy, making me wetter as he quickly removed his shirt, trousers, and briefs. I ran my tongue over my lips as I watched him grip his cock and climb on the bed. He settled between my thighs.

"Masturbate. I want to see how you pleasure yourself," Jonas said.

My skin heated. "I'm not comfortable doing that with you right here looking."

Jonas leaned down, kissed my thigh and smiled. "We'll do it together this time." He positioned himself behind me, his erection pressed against my ass as his arms circled my waist. His skin hot against my back. He opened me up and leaned his head over my shoulder, his warm breath coming in heavier as he focused in at the apex of my thighs and waited.

I trembled as I timidly moved my left hand and circled my finger around my clit, an unanticipated moan escaping.

"So sexy, Lily." Jonas's fingers followed the same path as my own. My eyes lidded and my breathing sped up as we circled, my fingers dipping down through my slick labia fast.

"That's right. Use me," he grunted. His fingers drove me faster as the coiling low on my body tightened.

Opening my legs wider, I took Jonas's fingers and put them to use, rubbing and pressing against me as I moaned and rocked against them. "Jonas. I'm. Coming. Jonas."

"Yes," he hissed. I cried out as I came. Breaking apart in his arms. He moved on top of me. The head of his cock just penetrated my sex. Grasping my arms, he secured them over my head before pushing inside me in one continuous hard thrust, making us both cry out.

"I can't be gentle right now," Jonas said roughly. "I need you to take it."

"Yes. I will," I said, though he probably wasn't looking for an answer. Using every muscle in his arsenal, he slammed his cock inside of me.

Arching to meet his need, I cried out as pain and pleasure filled me.

"Oh, Jonas." My voice wasn't one I recognized. Born from the sensation of his deep and fast penetration. I gazed up at him. Lidded eyes. His jaw clenched tight. Holding on, until his mouth went slack and he came. He kept thrusting and I joined him convulsing, my arms still trapped in his.

He kissed me and let go of my hands, then moved me to spoon against him. I was completely sated and exhausted, ready for sleep. To my surprise, Jonas joined me. He stirred hours later and I woke in his arms.

"Is it always like this?" I asked, closing my eyes.

"What? Sex?" Jonas asked.

"Yeah. Well. Never mind," I said. I moved away and

twirled the ends of my hair.

"Doesn't matter what it always is," Jonas said. "What matters is what you feel when we have sex together." Jonas turned my head and kissed me. "I should get some work done. I have some press coming up. Part of my self-promotion for the book everyone has been asking me to write and publish."

Yeah the book. I blushed. "Like me."

"Now *you*," he nuzzled my neck, "I don't mind a bit."

My brows came together. Because I already got a presentation out of him.

"What are you thinking about?" Jonas asked.

I smiled at him and relaxed my face, but decidedly didn't tell him. Instead, I said, "You're like a machine. Always working to do more. I admire that."

Jonas lowered his head and sighed. "I didn't have a choice, to be honest. It was the way I was brought up. My father chose every part of our lives. Planned it out from birth to death. Like all Cranes before him. Trinity School, then Harvard Business. My brother Vincent escaped, but not me."

My heart constricted as I saw raw emotion on his face. I pulled him to my breasts and he rested his head. "That must have been hard. Did you want to do it?"

He snuggled close. "I don't know. I believe it was now, but I never knew different. It was his expectation of me, and his expectation became everyone's around him. He wanted me to be him. A leader. I was raised to set the bar, and do whatever it took to stay on top."

"Yeah. Mathias Crane was renowned," I said stroking his hair. *So soft like silk.* "You too."

He exhaled. "When I was young in his business firm, he found out I let a friend get away with stealing a client. So he demoted me, and promoted him."

I frowned. "That's completely unfair. You must have been devastated."

Jonas looked up and gave me a small smile. He rubbed the skin between my brows until I stopped frowning. "He told me his 'fucking me over' proved he was smarter and more committed than me. After that, I worked harder and took every client away from that friend. I crushed his business. That earned me my first partnership."

I stroked the sides of his face. "That must have been so difficult."

Jonas leaned into my hand. "It was. I learned then that if you want to succeed, you put your work first. And do whatever it takes to attain success and keep it." He peered at me through a fan of thick lashes. So achingly beautiful, Jonas.

I kissed him and wrapped myself close, cuddle against his body. "That's harsh, but you were under a lot of pressure."

"I was," Jonas said quietly. "But it was my father's way. He didn't have any friends, just business. My mother divorced my father when I was nine. Or 'upgraded', as my dad put it, to his friend. A friend he crushed in business too, mind you. She put us in boarding school the second we could walk, so I didn't care or notice when she left, but that didn't work for my father. He needed to see her suffer for leaving him alone."

"Where is your mother now?" I asked gingerly.

He blinked. "She's in Connecticut, at a nursing home. She has early onset dementia. Doesn't even know or remember what she did." The raw emotion on his face made it difficult for me to sit by, but deep down I knew he needed to be heard. I leaned in and kissed him. He exhaled and was silent for a few minutes, but then continued.

"Dani made it so that Paul and I go see her. That's just how she is … was, with me. Followed me and led when I needed her to." He cleared his throat, "As for my father, after my mother left, he made sure he was never alone again. He made … arrangements with women." He flicked his eyes at me. "The only people that attended his funeral were me, Dani, and Paul," Jonas said. "Dani and I promised each other that Paul would make his own path. Follow his dreams. I want him to be better than my father … and me."

A pang went through my chest as I met his cloudy eyes. "I'm sorry for your father, but I don't believe you're like that."

"I am. I became him now, anyway," he said dully and sighed. "There you go again. Pulling me out of myself and getting me to share things I don't tell any-one." He rose up and clasped the sides of my face. "Only you, Lily. I don't know how, but you make it easy. I did with Dani too, I guess, but…." He gazed into my eyes intently. "Even after I told you how cruel I have been in business; you still look at me the same. Like I'm special."

"You *are* special, Jonas. You work hard and care for your family. You employ thousands of people through your companies. You work tirelessly to help educate those coming after you. You're caring, thoughtful, passionate, generous, and…."

He stopped me with a kiss. "So are you, Lily." A small smile playing on his lips. "Now enough about me. I would love to sketch you," he said.

I rubbed my eyes. "Now?"

"Yes." Jonas pecked my cheek then climbed off the bed, walking over to the closet and removing a sketchpad and a small box of art coals. He seemed almost shy as he made his way to the bed and sat back down and waited for an answer from me.

I grimaced. "My face?"

Jonas rubbed my leg. "Not just your face. All of you just as you are." He leaned down and kissed my inner thigh. "Beautiful and perfect."

I looked down and let my hair fall into my face. "I'm hardly perfect."

Jonas put the sketchpad down and climbed on top of me, kissing me passionately. "I think you are. And this means a lot to me."

I curled my chin under. "I guess, but…." I lifted up and tugged the sheet.

"If I give you some modesty. May I?" Jonas draped the sheet around me.

My chest fluttered as I watched the joy spread across his face at the possibility of sketching me and I knew instantly I would agree to keep it there. "Okay."

He smiled broadly. "Thank you."

Jonas maneuvered me on my side and back and became engrossed in his sketching. I tried to peer over to look at the pieces, but he stopped me.

"Wait until I'm done," he said.

I smiled and nodded at him as his eyes moved over the curves of my body while he sketched on his pad. When he was done, he climbed on the bed and presented the images to me. His drawings were beautiful and I could see that, but I could also see everything I wished to change about myself.

He sensed the shift in my mood, and put his pad and coals away and came back to the bed.

"What's wrong, Lily?" Jonas climbed in the bed next to me.

I averted my eyes and turned the corners of my mouth up. "Nothing. I'm tired."

Jonas frowned. "You're lying. You have that sad look again, but now you're trying to hide it," he said. "Did you dislike the sketches?"

I swallowed. I could tell he was guarded and I didn't want to hurt his feelings. "They're beautiful. I guess I wish … I don't know." I glanced over at the sketchpad. "*She* could be a little different."

Jonas captured my chin and lifted it up to him and studied me. "The sketches are not separate from you. You're beautiful. Your full breasts, your hips. Every piece of you," he said assuredly.

My bottom lip trembled. "Thank you," I said softy.

Jonas studied me, then said softly, "Oh, Lily."

What did he see? He didn't explain, but started kissing me and stroking his hands over my body. When I was completely desperate for him to fill me, he moved my legs open and pressed inside me. And though I knew it was my own personal demons, I moved my legs around him and admired his willingness to try to change my mind.

CHAPTER THIRTEEN

M Y DESK PHONE chimed, calling me back from the fog that had clouded my thoughts since I arrived at work this morning. "Lily Salome, how may I help you?" I said, using my professional voice.

"It's Olivia at reception," her tone musical. "You have a delivery."

"I'll be right down." Placing the phone back down, a grin spread across my face, chasing away the melancholy that had settled there since Jonas had dropped me off at Arch after our breakfast. *Our last night.* Jonas was leaving New York tomorrow morning. Although we shared a lot over the week, we hadn't yet discussed when he would return or if he wanted to continue our companionship.

Rising from my desk, I took the stairs down to the lobby and walked over to Olivia at the reception desk. Her big brown eyes were as wide as her smile when she motioned towards a pretty large bouquet of Tiger Lilies and dark truffles, which I opened right away and shared with her. I inhaled deeply the incredible scent of the flowers. They were beautiful and smelled incredible, just like the man I knew sent them to me, Jonas Crane.

I took the elevator back up and settled down at my cubicle before opening the card sticking out of the top.

Tiger Lilies for Tiger Lily.
Not nearly as beautiful as you.
Dinner reservations at 6:30 p.m. and La Traviata

Sucking in air as I read over the note, I waited for the pain to grip around my heart at the mention of my parents' nickname for me. A twinge was still there, but not the consuming dread that had at times paralyzed me. Was I finally letting go, or was it Jonas? Inhaling the aroma of the flowers and staring at the note, another tingle went through me. It had to be Jonas. Not only had he sent me flowers, he included an invitation to the opera and dinner tonight. He considered *me* a romantic? I beamed as I took my phone to text him after I placed the flowers on my desk.

I love the Tiger Lilies. You didn't tell me you were taking me to the opera tonight!

Right away, he texted me back. *It was a surprise. I'm glad you like your flowers. I'm looking forward to tonight too.*

I texted again. *How's work?*

He replied. *It's going well. I should have it all finished in time for my flight tomorrow.*

I sank back into my chair. After everything that had happened, I had almost forgotten he was flying away tomorrow. I didn't even know when I would see him again. We hadn't discussed the companionship since the first night. What would I do if he decided he didn't want to continue?

I found myself worrying over Jonas throughout the afternoon, and the distraction was making the simplest of tasks take twice as long. I wasn't getting any work done, so I decided to take the rest of the time off. I sent a message to Gregor, who was due back in town tomorrow evening.

Sounds good. Let's go to Sophie's tomorrow at 6:00 p.m.? I've got so much to share with you.

I texted him back. *Sounds good. See you tomorrow. Thanks.*

I sent a quick message to Jonas. *Leaving work early. Are you at the hotel?*

Jonas sent a texted back. *I'll send David to pick you up in 30 minutes.*

I texted in turn. *No need. I'm out the door. I'll be there soon.*

I closed my cell and quickly packed the rest of my things. I waited a few minutes, but didn't get a response to my message. I walked down the street and around the corner, flagging down the first taxi I saw. I was rounding 51st and Lexington in under twenty minutes. I paid the taxi and walked into the Waldorf Astoria Hotel. It wasn't until I approached the door and heard the elevated voices that I started to feel alarmed. I knocked on the door and everything went silent. *Is everything alright?*

I pressed the door button.

"I'll answer it," a young male voice sung out. Before I had a chance think about it, the door swung open and a tall muscular young male with an angular shaped face, thick black hair, and sea blue eyes stared at me with a mischievous grin on his full lips. He was a younger version of Jonas. His son Paul?

I lifted my brows. "Excuse me, I'm, Ms. Lily Salomé."

"Now I understand what Mom's talking about," he said and motioned widely for me to come in as I reluctantly crossed inside the suite. My eyes met Jonas, who was standing by the couch with a grim expression on his face.

"This is my rude son, Paul." Jonas folded his arms.

"You cut in on our father and son time," Paul said curtly to me.

My cheeks warmed. "I'm sorry. I'll go."

Paul laughed hardily. "You're hot when you blush."

"Paul," Jonas hissed, "apologize. Now."

"No sense of humor," Paul said. He sidestepped Jonas. "Sorry, Lily. You're prettier than his past girlfriends and his latest in Texas."

I felt the blood drain from my face. "Girlfriends?"

"That's it. Consider that snowboarding weekend cancelled," Jonas barked.

Paul rolled his eyes. "Not like you to overreact, Dad." He walked over and picked up his coat from the back of the couch. He winked at me. "I need a date to the dance in a couple of weeks. Just putting it out there." He chuckled and strolled out the door.

"I'll be back," Jonas called out on his heels. After

about ten minutes, he returned to the room.

I touched my warm face. "Well, that didn't exactly go well."

Jonas groaned and then combed his fingers through his hair. "Paul decided to skip his afternoon classes and surprise me. He loves to get a rise, which I'm afraid will probably get worse than better. I apologize for his behavior."

I frowned. "What did he mean about your latest girlfriend in Texas?" He walked over to me and took my bag out of my hands and walked to the closet.

"I had a companion in Texas, but we're back to being friends again," Jonas said, matter-of-factly.

I walked over to the couch and sat down. "So you date and have sex with them, then push them back to friends? I'm confused."

Jonas walked over and sat down next to me. "I'm not ready for a commitment, and we made better friends. So yes. She was a companion and now she's a friend."

I frowned. "It's just more than I ever experienced before."

"I know," he said slowly. "Which is why I hesitated in offering companionship to you." He took my hand and faced me, and a tingling sensation went through me. "Are you having second thoughts? I know I want this to continue after I leave tomorrow."

I stared at his handsome face and saw desire and a hint of uncertainty. This powerful man seemed just as confused about what was happening between us as I was about him. I wanted the pleasure. I needed it. I needed him. "No, I'm not. I just find it all a bit overwhelming. But I do want to continue our companionship." I opened my arms. He took me in, pressing his body against mine and kissing me.

I moved back from him. "What did Paul mean by Dani?"

His mouth curved. "Dani thinks fondly of you and she has been talking about you."

My eyes widened. "Really? I barely talked to her."

He placed his finger under my chin and lifted. "Like me, she goes by her instincts." He gazed at me warmly, melting my insides. I glanced down at his lips and he leaned in and gave me a chaste kiss. "Let's take a shower and get dressed. I want you bare under your dress tonight." He stood up and held out his hand.

"This suite has two bathrooms," I said, stalling.

"Yes," he said with a glint of amusement on his face.

I swallowed and took his hand, happy he hadn't asked me to spell out my meaning.

He reached in and turned on the shower once we reached the bathroom. I turned my back to him, and my fingers jittered as I struggled to unbutton my shirt. My insecurities raced through my mind. I jolted as Jonas pressed his body behind me and eased his hands around my waist.

"I know this is difficult for you, but think about what we shared. I love your body and I want to see you," he said quietly. My heart stuttered at his understanding of how years of insecurities wouldn't be solved in a few days. It then dawned on me that he was working with me to create new memories, and that touched me deeply, quickening my resolve as he took over removing my clothing. I stared up into his eyes and focused on what was before me. Desire was evident as his gaze wandered freely over my form, his mouth lowering to kiss and suckle my breasts as he removed my bra. His fingers teased my pussy as he removed my panties. I reached out and explored his body, moving over the solid plains of his chest and down to his thick cock, now engorged and the tip glistening with pre-cum. I bent down and moaned as I licked off the salty sweetness.

"Come here, beautiful," Jonas pulled me up and into his arms and kissed me deeply, then guided us inside the shower. The steam surrounded us as the warm water beat down on our bodies. He maneuvered me forward until the cold tile hit my back. "Give me your leg," Jonas instructed, holding his hand out. I balanced my hands on his shoulders as I lifted my leg and he grabbed a hold of it, bending at the knee as he lined up his cock to my slick entrance and dipped the head in. We both groaned loudly at our joining. The sensations fired off in utter bliss.

"Don't move," he gritted as he held my leg and hip tightly, setting a slow pace. With every roll of his hips, he sunk his cock deeper, angling it to massage my clit as he drove this torturous ride to ecstasy. The pressure at my core was so intense that I grunted, and Jonas was right there with me. Our eyes connected and the surge of electricity sparked between us. I realized we were synced, riding the edge to oblivion. As he lifted me higher, he plunged deeper than he had ever been before and I yelled as I came hard, my whole body tremoring against him. Jonas followed after me, crying out my name in his release. A sob crawled up my throat as another orgasm rocked my body.

I wrapped my other leg around him, clinging to him as if he was my last lifeline. His hand stroked down my back and he held on, keeping our connection. After a little while, Jonas eased me down to my feet and I leaned up to kiss his lips. He stroked his hands down my face, but didn't say anything, just started washing me. I was calmly sated and didn't oppose as his hands roamed freely over my body. For the moment, I savored the feeling of being more than his companion; of belonging to him completely.

Once we were finished, he set me down on my feet and we walked back into the bedroom, where we went about changing for the performance and dinner. As I returned to the bathroom to get dressed, I decided to forego Jonas's request for no panties. I just felt too naked without them. In a strapless bra, garters, and silk nylons, the ensemble would surely still appeal to him.

The black velvet cocktail dress was one I had worn to the symphony a few years ago, but still appeared current. I polished off my look with my long black hair up in a twist, cursing myself for not calling Dee for a quick hair appointment.

As I was putting on my red lip balm, I caught a glimpse of Jonas standing in the doorway in his immaculate black suit and felt a tightening low on my body. He looked drop dead gorgeous. He grinned as he walked up to me.

"You look stunning, Lily." He bent down and kissed my cheek. "You keep looking at me like that, and we'll have to stay here." I put all my feelings into my face.

He hesitated, then kissed my forehead. "Let's go," he said quietly.

I sighed and nodded. He walked us out and collected our coats, helping me into mine, then we headed out the door.

The Lincoln center wasn't too far from Waldorf Astoria. Jonas helped me out the car and I felt like a child at an amusement park. I had seen the opera house many times in films, but to be here was simply magical. As Jonas pressed the small of my back, I stood transfixed by the grand fountain out front of the hall.

He had to practically tug me away to steer me towards the walls of windows, before the stone center. As we crossed the threshold, I took in the immense ornamental balustrades and the crystal chandeliers in the auditorium. It was a spectacle of the senses and I was transformed along with the crowd hall of people dressed in their finest for the performance.

"We have reservations," Jonas said as he steered me through the crowd and towards the entrance of the

Grand Tier Restaurant. We barely paused at the entrance before we were escorted to a table overlooking the courtyard of the center. As I took the seat next to Jonas, my lips formed a wide grin. "I can't believe you arranged this."

"To tell you the truth, I have season tickets," he said. "We used to, well, *I* used to, drag Dani along."

I giggled. "My dad and I dragged my mother. In fact, she would fall asleep at Tanglewood Festival. Give her a fiddle and a washboard and she was in heaven." It was at that moment the waitress came by and Jonas ordered salad and filet au sole for me and beef tenderloin for himself and a bottle of wine.

Jonas ordered for me without asking again, but I didn't mind as I was completely distracted by the ambiance.

I took a sip of my wine. They brought the Arugula and endive salads. "My parents met through a fundraiser for the art camp I mentioned before."

"Perchance to Dream, the Salomé' Love Legacy," Jonas said and winked at me.

I beamed at him. He remembered. "Yes. She sent out letters for performers and one letter had serendipitously reached my father."

"A serendipitous letter, I like that," Jonas grinned.

I smiled and ate my salad, then said, "My dad showed up with his viola and my mom said to him, 'So what can you do with that fiddle.'"

Jonas exhaled. "That must have ruffled him," he said.

I giggled. "Yep. He told her he was a Principal viola with the Boston Symphony." I did my best impression of my father's prideful voice. "He set out to edify her error and played a piece for her. She responded by telling him, 'You'll do.'" Jonas laughed. We finished our salad and our main dishes were served.

I moaned as the filet practically melted in my mouth.

"I like that sound, but I think the scream in the car was better," Jonas said.

I flushed for him. "I can't look at David anymore."

"Don't worry about him." Jonas smirked. "He's seen and heard worse."

I scrunched my face. I didn't want to hear about Jonas with someone else. "You pig."

His eyes flashed and he lifted his chin. "I didn't mean me. David has a life outside of driving me around you know."

I casted my eyes down and took a sip of my wine. "Oh. Right. Apologies."

"So what did your father say about your mother's response to him?" he asked, smiling at me.

I beamed. "Oh, my father said, 'She was so beautiful, I didn't care about her silly pouting, I fell in love with her.' And they married soon after." My voice broke.

He reached over and squeezed my hand. "It's my favorite story."

"Thank you for sharing it with me," Jonas said softly.

My smile quivered a little. "Thank you for tonight."

"Dani enjoyed the opera, but preferred a Ravi Shankar or something with an Eastern flair. She was the inspiration for our trek through Kenya and trips to India."

I sipped my wine then said, "I read about that in your last interview with Time Magazine. What was it like?"

He tilted his head in thought as he sipped his drink. "Thrilling, challenging, and remarkable. I'm happy I did that, but not on my list for the future." We went back to our meals and finished. The waiter came by. "They are seating now, Mr. Crane."

Jonas paid for the dinner ignoring my feeble attempt at offering to split the cost.

I licked my lips. "So, what is on your list for the future?"

He held out his hand to me. "Enjoying the opera with you, Tiger Lily."

I looked down. "Don't call me that," I mumbled.

He trailed his hand down my arm, sending a shiver through me. "I enjoyed hearing the story behind it and I believe it suits you."

My stomach fluttered as he took my elbow and steered me towards the balcony and our box for the opera.

As the curtain went up, Jonas took my hand and held on to it throughout the three acts of the performance. I sat in awe of the scenes, the swell of the arias, and the beauty of the hall. It was as if we had gone back in time. Part of me wished it would never end, as the finale marked an end of the night and the beauty of his company.

Jonas squeezed my hand during the final scene of Violetta and Giuseppe's reunion, and in that moment a flutter went through my chest. I swiped under my eye pondering why falling in love was so painful. Picking up on my somber mood, Jonas rubbed gently on my hand.

I swallowed hard as we rose, and walked down the stairs and out of the hall. "Thank you."

Jonas took out his cell and kept my hand as we walked to the car and once inside, wrapped his arm around me. So oddly familiar and natural his touch and care of me.

"So what did you think?" Jonas asked.

I leaned my head against his shoulder. "I hadn't allowed myself to enjoy an opera in a long time, it was like meeting an old friend."

He tilted my face up and kissed me deeply, caressing his tongue with mine.

"I've wanted to do that all evening," Jonas said softly. "And this." Jonas moved me to lay back on the seat. He reached under my dress and when he touched my mound, he stilled. Lifting my dress higher, his eyes iced over as he glared down at the black-laced panties underneath.

I giggled. "I wondered how long it would take for you to find out."

"I told you not to wear panties." Jonas stared down pressing his lips together. He let go of my thighs and pulled my dress back in place and sat away from me.

What was his problem? I stared at him in disbelief. My mouth dropped open and I frowned. "I thought it was funny."

"It's not the panties. It's more my expectation of you. I used them as, I had hoped, a fun way to help communicate that to you," he said curtly.

Even though I had Jonas brooding and his reaction was in my view an over-reaction, I was aroused. So much so that my clit throbbed. The more I sat, the further the intensity. I found myself reaching up under my skirt to seek sexual release.

Jonas grabbed my hand. "You will not." Shockingly, he went as far as lowering the dividing window between us and the front seat of the car. Knowing me well enough to know that I wouldn't do anything in front of David.

I dropped my hands and grimaced at him.

Jonas just sat there stoically, completely ignoring me.

My anger started to dissipate the more I stared at him. Would he stay angry? Would he want me to leave? "It was a joke. I'll play along now."

"I know you will," Jonas said tersely, still not looking at me. "Now let's sit here and enjoy the remainder of our ride. We'll discuss this when we get back to the suite."

Crossing my arms, I turned my head and glared out the window and said nothing.

The few blocks remaining had been the longest I had experienced in my life. Jonas had not relented, even when we pulled up to the curb of the hotel. Climbing out of the car, I was relieved when he splayed his hand on my lower back and moved us through the hotel and up to his suite, though he still didn't look at or say one word to me.

My stomach started to churn. "What can I do to end this?" I hunched over when we reached the door and he closed it behind us.

Jonas folded his arms and finally spoke, "Strip off your clothing, place your heels in the closet, then fold everything else neatly and hand them to me."

My heart pounded as I glanced up at him and saw his expression was stern. There was no doubt that Jonas not only expected his command to be followed, but promptly. I reached to my back and unzipped my dress, then removed my heels and put them away, all the time glancing towards him. He walked through the room turning on every light, exposing me. My fingers fumbled as I removed my dress and unhooked my bra, then rolled down the thigh highs. After folding them, I shook as I lifted them up and held them out in front of him.

"Stand here." Jonas took them from me and placed them on the table. He put his things away, then returned in front of me.

I trembled as my mind played over Declan ignoring me and withholding affection after my parents died. The agony of working to be his "good girl" and earn his physical and emotional affection. *I can't go through that again.* I crumbled down on the floor and wrapped my arms around myself in comfort. "I'm sorry," I said nasally. Then a tear fell, and another. Before I knew it, I was sobbing.

"Lily." Jonas quickly scooped me up off the floor and carried me to the bedroom. He moved me to straddle his lap and held me close, rubbing my back.

I closed my eyes. "I'm sorry. Please don't ignore me, hold me."

"I know you are sorry, and I'm not going to let you go," Jonas kissed my forehead, "but I need to know why you're crying. I didn't expect this reaction. Talk to me."

I took a deep breath and told him. "I guess you want me to go now," I said desolately. "I'm more complicated than you signed up for."

"I could kill him," Jonas said angrily, understanding reaching his eyes. He cupped my face. "I'd never do that to you." He saw my doubt, so he continued. "I'll work to earn that trust from you in time. But what I do want you to know is that I don't want you to go. I want to know your thoughts and feelings." He lifted my chin and gazed into my eyes. "I find you impossible to ignore and irresistible to touch."

I blinked. "But. In the car … I like you leading. I want you to, but I didn't understand. I needed to know." I bit my lip as I tried to find the words, "I needed…."

"Discussion. Assurance," Jonas offered and I nodded.

He stroked the side of my face and chin. "Well, I like control and you told me that you like to be led. So I pushed for more of it, but now I know that was too much too soon, especially after what happened to you. I should have discussed this with you and I apologize for that."

My insides warmed and I leaned up and kissed him. "I accept. I enjoy your sexual control and I don't want that to end. I just need to know how you feel about me and what we're doing so I can go with your demands. Does that make sense?"

"Yes. Rest assured that I do like you, Lily, and I also enjoy controlling you in here." Jonas kissed my lips tenderly. I pressed my lips harder against his and our kiss deepened. It was then I realized again I was nude in his lap, while he was still in his shirt and slacks.

Jonas broke off and inhaled sharply as his eyes roved over my body and back up to my eyes, waiting for him.

He showed me his desire, and heat flooded me once more. My breathing became heavier as my nipples swelled. The pulsing throb of my sex came back to life. I leaned in and kissed his lips, down his jaw and chin yet Jonas remained still. What did he want? What did I want? I wanted him in the way he wanted to be with me. The way we both wanted to be with each other. So I tilted back and said, "Don't hold back."

Jonas kissed me lightly on the mouth. "Good." He moved me on the bed and stripped off his clothing.

"Move on your knees and lift your ass up, arms at your side," he commanded.

I took a deep breath and moved into the position he requested of me, letting my arms rest at my sides and my legs fold under me. The vulnerability of the position didn't go unnoticed by me.

Jonas moved behind me and stroked my sex, gently. Over and over my sensitive flesh, heightened by arousal, but not enough to sate me. I moaned and lifted my hips in hope of gaining more pressure, but he abruptly stopped and caressed my back. No words to me, his actions spoke for him. He wanted the control, but wouldn't deny me affection. My heart squeezed as I waited for him to continue to seek what he needed of me.

He started again, slow teasing strokes of my labia and clit, making me swell and ache in need of release. Groaning, he rubbed his hard cock against my swollen pussy, brushing the head right up against my clit. Sweat broke out over my body as the sensations jolted through me. I tried to remain still in hopes he would push me over, but my body pushed back, seeking him to fill me. The second I did, Jonas stopped and removed his cock, rubbing my back once more. My body hummed, longing for what he held away from me. When I started coming down, he began rubbing his cock against my sensitive flesh again.

"Jonas," I whispered.

He kissed my back. "Not yet, Lily." He kept up his punishing rub, and I shook and panted under him as I fought to give what he needed of me.

Finally, I felt the tip of his cock from the back as he entered me. Pressing hot inside me, and I could have wept. I bit my lip against the fullness and pressure as my inner walls stretched to take all of him. The sensation was more pleasure than anything I ever felt before. Breathing in and out fast, I shook as I waited for him to lead me.

Gripping my hips with his hands, Jonas thrust his dick in and out of me. The sensation was incredible and my sex clenched, right on the cusp of an orgasm.

Jonas picked up the pace and hissed as he came, emptying inside of me. He rubbed his fingers against the sides of my clit. "Come." Swiveling and grinding his cock inside me as he stroked me with the pressure I needed, and I came convulsing under his touch.

"Jonas," I cried out.

Turning me over, he kissed over my face and gazed at me. The warmth radiating out of his eyes filled my chest. He kissed a path to my breasts and suckled them. I ran my hands through the silky strands of his hair. Oh, how I wanted this man.

"Open your legs," he said.

I complied, this time without hesitation, ready to take what he wanted of me. He rewarded me by kissing down my mound and licking my pussy. "Come." And I did. For him. For us.

Turning me over, he grasped my sex possessively, covering me with his hard body as he ground against me until I thrashed and came under him again. I sunk into the warmth and control he had of me. His body completely enveloped me.

He kept his hand on my sex as if conveying a message for me: as his companion, this was his and his alone.

I pressed in to his grip with my own determination. *Yes. Yours. Take it. Take me.*

CHAPTER FOURTEEN

I WOKE AND glared at the side clock. 6:30 a.m. My mind was heavy on Jonas's pending departure. I was captivated by him, and couldn't help but want more of his company. I knew my thoughts were dangerous, but I always went with my heart.

His need to control me should have put me off, but it didn't. He had somehow wrapped me so close to him that I was having a hard time dealing with the idea that he would be leaving. I turned over and watched him sleep. I could make out the plains of his muscular body through the light of dawn peeking through the sides of the curtains in the bedroom. I looked at his cock and felt a stirring low on my body. I had never been so aroused before and wanted more of him. It was like I didn't just have sex with him only hours earlier.

"Lily," Jonas mumbled sleepily. He rolled on top of me, I moved his cock to my pussy and he slicked it against my arousal, the head brushing against my clit.

My eyes lidded as I moaned rocking against him. "Mmm."

Jonas moaned and pushed inside of me and started a slow thrust. I lifted my hips to take him deeper.

I let out a gasp at the feel of his cock massaging my channel as he ground his hips against me.

"So good inside you." He picked up speed and thrust faster inside me, until he came, yelling out above me. He rubbed his fingers against my clit, continuing to move his cock until my orgasm hit me and I withered as I held on tightly to him. Saying his name, I kissed across his chest.

He kissed the top of my head. "I don't know how I'm going to leave today," he whispered.

We both knew he would. He fell back to sleep, and I eased out from under him and out of the bed. I went to the bathroom and had a quick shower, and put on my clothing for my casual workday, denim jeans and blue turtleneck.

I had a thought on what to get him to remember me, but what do you give a man that has everything? I sighed as I packed my backpack. When I reached the closet, I found my dress, freshly dry cleaned hanging there.

I grinned. *Jonas, ever considerate*. I took out a pair of panties, took off a ribbon from the basket, and tied a bow.

I walked over to the desk and wrote a short note.

I know this is may seem silly, but I hope you appreciate the gesture.

Thank you for the last few days. Tiger Lily.

Jonas suddenly appeared in the room in his robe, his gaze seeking me. My breath caught as I took in his beauty. I pondered how long he would have that effect on me.

Whether he noticed me in his briefcase, he didn't acknowledge. "I'm going to get dressed. Breakfast should be here any minute," Jonas said, then turned and went inside the bathroom.

The door sounded and I went to open it, flushing as the waiter smiled broadly at me and went about setting up the table. Eggs benedict, hollandaise, winter fruit, and coffee. Jonas came out in a robe and signed the sheet, then went back inside the bathroom. The pull to go back in there with him was great, but I held myself back in self-preservation.

Jonas returned after a few minutes dressed as casually as I had ever seen him, a black shirt and denim jeans. His black hair was messy, sweeping across his forehead. His eyes fixed on me as he closed the distance and pressed a kissed to my lips and beyond, filling my mouth with the taste of mint.

"Did you sleep well?" Jonas asked as he poured us coffee.

I nodded, my throat closed to speech. I ate a few bites of the eggs and sipped the coffee.

"Thank you for everything," I said, my voice sounding thick.

Jonas put his fork down and opened his arms and I immediately stood and let him place me on his lap and cuddled me.

"Lily, I'm finding this difficult too," He said slowly, as he stroked my back.

He was? I let my head rest on his shoulder and inhaled his fresh scent.

He kissed the side of my face. "I'll be back in New York after going to Texas and a short trip to Seattle. I want to see you again."

I nodded. "I want that too."

Jonas fed me and him our breakfast and then stood me on my feet.

"I have a surprise for you." Jonas walked out of the room and into the bedroom and rolled in a black leather designer trolley bag.

My eyes dilated and I shook my head. "Jonas no. You shouldn't have."

Jonas pressed his lips together. "It's done and it's here. Do you like it?"

I stood and walked over to him and leaned up and kissed his lips. "Yes. But—"

"Then that's all that matters," he said, cutting me off. The corners of his mouth turned up. Before I could respond, the door sounded. He strolled over and David was there, along with a bell person to collect our things.

"Pumpkin time," I muttered.

Jonas held my hand as we walked out the door and to the elevator, through the lobby, check out, and to the door of his Bentley. He pulled me into his arms and held onto me all the way from the Waldorf Astoria to the

Arch building. These actions were more than I had ever imagined a companion would be, but I didn't protest. I wanted and needed it and he was willing to give it to me.

My breathing labored as the door opened. I had managed to hold it together up until we stopped.

"David will take you home tonight. So you don't need to bring anything," Jonas said.

I shook my head. "I have a work dinner with Gregor."

His jaw tightened. "Where?"

I bit my lip. "Gregor usually drops me …." The words died on my lips as the tension rose between us. "Sophie's."

Jonas turned and gave instructions to David, who nodded to me. "I want you safe, and knowing David will take you home eases me."

My insides warmed. *He cares.* I didn't have the time to think on it though.

I curled my chin under and waved. "Thank you. Jonas. Thanks for everything."

"Let me walk you inside," Jonas said tucking my hair behind my ear, then stroking down my neck.

I chewed my lip. "No, I think I will fall apart if you do."

Jonas sighed. He kissed my cheek. "We'll continue our conversation tonight."

I plastered a smile and looked up at him. "Yes. I look forward to it."

He gasped, then kissed me lightly on the lips.

"Thank you for your smile, Tiger Lily."

I lifted my brows. "No Shakespeare?" I joked.

He stared intently at me and didn't say anything for a few heartbeats.

He then whispered, "I'll have something for you tonight."

I licked my lips and said, "Parting is such sweet sorrow—"

"That I shall say goodnight till tomorrow. Let's discuss that tonight." Jonas kissed me again, this time crushing his lips to mine.

When we broke apart, I giggled. "Public affection from Jonas Crane."

Jonas leaned against my forehead and breathe in. "I'm finding you impossible to resist." he said softly, then kissed my cheek.

My eyes filled, and I dropped my head. What was I doing?

He pulled me in a tight embrace. "I feel it too, Lily," he soothed. "I'll call you tonight." He winked at me then climbed inside the car.

Covering my mouth, I watched his car pull off down the street. He was gone and I wasn't sure when I would see him again. Once the car turned the corner, I walked inside the office and ran straight into the bathroom. Locking myself inside a stall, I sunk down on the seat and cried.

CHAPTER FIFTEEN

ONCE I WAS empty, I numbly splashed water on my face and walked back to my desk. I turned on the computer and sent off a few emails to some of our clients. Taking an extra fifteen minutes over lunch, I made it to black light spin class at the corporate gym. The vigorous exercise combined with the blaring techno music helped to quiet my thoughts and worries over when I might see Jonas again. Halfway through the chicken salad I brought back to eat at my desk, my phone chimed. My pulse increased as I sought to pick it up, but in my hurry managed to drop it on the floor. Calm down. Picking it up, I sighed as I looked at the name on display and answered. Gregor.

"Can I tell you who the star at the conference was?" Gregor trilled.

I groaned, then laughed in the phone. "You were, and I'm not surprised. No one works a room like you."

"That's what was missing from this conference. I was Conan without Andy. I should have taken you along with me."

I played with the ends of my hair. "Perhaps next time."

"I'm getting ready to board. I'll be at the office at 6:00. Would you mind calling Sophie's?"

I smiled. "Done. I did that a few days ago."

"Great. I'm up for a few cocktails to celebrate. We can afford our car service to take you back to Jersey tonight. They are calling us to board."

"That's alright, I have a ride home. See you soon." I hung up.

I looked at the clock. Jonas would be landing in a few hours. Would he call me? I hated the need that arose in me. Turning back to my computer, I tried to throw myself back into work.

I finally turned my computer off at 6:00 p.m. Gregor would be here any minute to collect me. I ran my hands down my shirt and jeans. My mind turned to Jonas. He had landed at least four hours ago, but he hadn't sent me a text or called me. I worried over our morning and last night. Was I too clingy last night? Did he decide I wasn't mature enough for him? A weirdness pressed in my chest at the thought of not hearing from him again.

"Lily." I was so lost in thought that I didn't realize Gregor had come and was standing behind me. I turned around to face him and smiled. He was just as messy as me, in his grey pullover and denim jeans. My brow raised at the trim to his loose hanging bob and the weird look on his face as his green eyes met mine.

Gregor cursed and folded his arms. "You had sex

with him already?" His voice went up at the end, and I felt bad.

My skin burned as I struggled to school my face. "What? How did you … I'm. Yes." I dropped my head.

He tugged my ponytail. "We'll talk about it."

I shook my head. "I don't want to talk about it."

"I'll buy you a Long Island Iced Tea and we'll talk about it," Gregor said. Then he took a breath. "I need to talk to you about it."

"What, so you can make me feel bad?" My voice was small and I rubbed my stomach.

"I'm not trying to shame you," Gregor said diplomatically. "I just know you and I know him. So I think you need some perspective."

I shutdown my computer. "Okay." Standing, I picked up my phone and placed it in my handbag. As I was putting on my coat, my phone chimed alerting me that I had a new text message. I beamed in delight as I read the screen. *Jonas Crane.*

The second I got here I got pulled into meetings.

I sighed in relief.

"I'll be right back," Gregor said, walking to his office.

"Okay," I called, then went back to my text and quickly replied.

I thought about you all day. Did you find anything out of the ordinary in your case?

A new text came in before I could put my phone away. I grinned as I read his message, hearing his voice in my mind.

Oh yes. I will have to show you just how much I appreciated it the next time I'm in town.

When will that be? I replied.

I stared at the screen until Gregor came back from his office and motioned for me to follow him. I fell in place and we took the elevator to the ground floor and walked out the building. My phone finally beeped and I looked at it as we walked down the street.

A couple of weeks. Possibly less.

I sighed.

Okay. I have dinner with Gregor now. I'll talk to you later?

"It's rude to text on your phone the whole time," Gregor quipped. I exhaled and fell back into step.

Yes. David will be there until you leave. Talk to you later.

As we approached the white brick and glass building that housed Sophie's, I spotted David and Jonas's Bentley. *He's so considerate.* I beamed as I waved to David, then followed Gregor inside the bar restaurant. The host set us at a small cloth table. Gregor pulled back my cushy beige and dark wood chair and took the seat across from me. The place was not as full as it would be in an hour with a steady flow of the after-work suit crowd walking in and settling near the oak bar upfront. The cedar flooring and oversized seating gave it a lounge atmosphere. A waitress came over and took our order. We both ordered burgers and Long Island Iced Teas. When she walked away, Gregor turned to me and blew out.

"I saw the car. So tell me what happened?" Gregor asked.

I flushed and shrugged. "Well, it's nothing really.

Just casual. That's it."

The waitress brought over our drinks and we both sipped for a few minutes.

"I'm not mad at you for having sex," Gregor said, sipping his drink. "I'm worried about what you might think it means."

I lifted my chin, ignoring the knot in my chest. "I'm not thinking it means anything." I refolded the napkin in my lap.

Gregor sighed. "Good. As I said I know Jonas and Dani. Well, I knew them back in college."

I shrugged. "So you were friends?"

"We were acquaintances. But I introduced them both to Maggie, my girlfriend. They in turn invited her into their inner circle of friends," he explained.

I bit my lip. "Not you?" He shook his head. "That's awful."

Gregor frowned. "It gets worse. Maggie broke up with me to pursue a sexual relationship with them. Talking some bullshit about being polyamorous, a word I doubt she even understood."

My brows rose. Jonas had mentioned their sexual relationship and Dani had alluded to as much at the yoga center. Still I was skeptical of Gregor's assessment of Maggie's decision. "That's harsh. Give her some credit she was a college student. She knew what it meant or she wouldn't have pursued it. Right?"

"Okay. Yeah. So I'm bitter, sue me," Gregor grumbled as he sucked down his drink. "I haven't seen many

woman like her. Beautiful face, hour glass figure, innocent, sweet…."

My lips parted. Dani had mentioned I looked a little
like a Maggie they knew. So maybe I was Jonas's type. "Is
that why you sent me?"

"Yes," Gregor said without hesitation. He tucked his
hair behind his ears. "But that's not the point. I thought
I was going to marry her. They eventually dumped her,
but when I came back to her afterwards, she didn't want
me. Said I couldn't give her what she needed. They
corrupted her."

The waitress came back and dropped off our burgers
and fries. Gregor bit into his and groaned in pleasure.

I picked at my burger with my fork. "I'm sorry,
Gregor. But maybe people change over time."

Gregor nodded. "I was willing to keep an open mind
about the polyamorous thing too. But she finally told me
the truth," he said between bites. "She didn't want
someone that didn't have the wealth and power they
had." He sipped his drink.

I looked down. "Oh. I'm sorry."

"Maggie was poor and they seduced her with sex and
gifts. Then, they dumped her. She was fun, but Dani and
Jonas were basically destined since birth. She had the
breeding, bank, and connections. Maggie thought she
was special to them. She thought they would still make
room for her in their lives," Gregor said.

My stomach churned as I listened and ate my burger.
"So, Jonas and Dani did what?"

"They not only dumped her, they took all their lavish lifestyle and friendly connections with them. Maggie was devastated to put it mildly, but she couldn't deal with going back to a regular guy like me," Gregor said. "So what I want you to know is, Jonas will enjoy you, but don't get hung up on him."

I put the burger down. Was that my fate? Would I become entranced with Jonas and his life, only to be heartbroken like Maggie? "I didn't know. They both seemed kind to me," I mumbled.

"Jonas isn't usually a liar. He didn't promise you anything, did he?" Gregor asked.

I moved the fries around my plate. "No. He didn't…."

Gregor shook his head. "You're already upset. I'll have a talk with him."

My eyes widened. "I'm not upset. I'm fine. Please, don't."

Gregor pursed his lips. "Sure you aren't." He sighed as he reached out and clasped my hand, "I just don't want to see you hurt. You're my favorite assistant. I like to see your face smiling."

I eased my hand back and busied myself twirling my straw around the inside of my now half empty glass. Trying to understand the Jonas, Dani, and Gregor experience from the ones I met. Surely people change over the years. I'm not the same as I was in Quincy. Of course, I was willing to make excuses because I liked them.

"Well," he said breaking our silence, "we have a good six weeks or so before our presentation with him."

I nodded. "Yes."

Gregor smiled broadly. "That will earn you a promotion. I may even be able to swing a raise now with all the business I generated during the conference."

"Great," I said, plastering on a smile.

Gregor joked over the remainder of the meal and I tried to be as enthusiastic for him as I could while he talked about his conference and all the new business contacts he made there. However, my mind was playing over the highlights of his conversation regarding Jonas.

I rubbed my chest and pushed the food away from me. He was right. Jonas hadn't promised me a relationship. We had a business companionship. The moments of him holding me; his comfort and care meant something to me, but not to him. I needed to not allow myself to get lost in him.

When the check arrived, we were both buzzed. I reached in my purse and took out my half.

He smiled jovially. "It's a business expense." We walked to the door and as we reached the Bentley and the car service I had set up for him to take back home. He opened his arms and I gave him a hug, and he held me.

"You take such good care of me," Gregor said. "You're special, Lily."

I moved back from him and he leaned down and kissed me.

I jumped back and touched my lips. "Gregor. What are you doing?"

His eyes widened. "Oh. I'm sorry. I ... don't be mad."

I rolled my eyes. "Go sleep it off." I suddenly found David at my side, blocking Gregor. "You need some help, Lily?"

"No. He was just joking around," I said. He didn't move from between us.

Gregor glared at David and moved towards his car. "I'll see you tomorrow, Lily. Remember what I said."

I shook my head as he stumbled in his car. "Light weight," I called out.

Turning back to David, I thanked him and climbed inside the car.

After a few minutes on the road, my phone chimed. I looked at the caller ID and a flutter went through my stomach. *Jonas.*

"I want to hear it from you," He barked out.

I narrowed my brows. *He's upset?* "You have David spying on me?"

"I have David looking out for you as you're alone in New York. What happened?" His harsh tone alerted me that David must have told him what happened between me and Gregor.

"Gregor was drunk. He didn't mean anything. It was just one kiss."

"I don't want any part of Gregor Worton touching you, or anyone else for that matter. I'll be clear when I talk to him."

My mouth went dry. "Don't, please. He's my friend and I know he didn't mean anything by it. He's probably all upset at himself now."

"Not open for discussion. He won't touch you again. Ever," he said sharply.

I glared at the phone. "Why not? I'm just a companion."

"*My* companion, which means you're mine and off limits to anyone but me," Jonas said.

I licked my lips as my stomach fluttered at the thrill of his possessiveness towards me. But I didn't liked the idea of Jonas fighting with Gregor. "He's my boss. I can't have you ordering him to not touch me."

"I'll just let him know he wouldn't have gotten into that conference in the Hamptons if it hadn't been for me," he said.

My brows furrowed as my mouth gaped. "Jonas, you didn't. How could you do that to him?"

"I helped him out. Arch is a good company, but let's be serious. He needed to be invited into the game to play. I made it happen. That's all."

I pushed back my hair as my heart sped up. "I'm not a bargaining piece. You can't go around threatening to take things away because of a kiss. That's insane."

"The second you let someone get away with disrespecting you, that respect is gone forever. There will be no compromise. Gregor knows that much about me," he said.

I frowned. "Please don't hurt him. He's one of my only friends." My words stumbled as a pain gripped my chest. Did I say too much?

"Shhh. I don't want you upset." His voice softened, "Please calm down. I'm not going to harm him, but we'll talk."

I pinched the bridge of my nose. "The talking is what concerns me."

"Answer me this. Did Gregor talk about me with you this evening?" Jonas asked.

I chewed my lip. "A little." It wasn't exactly a lie.

"A little," Jonas said curtly.

My stomach churned. "Okay, Jonas. But I like my job there. And I don't want to lose it."

"You won't," Jonas said with conviction.

We were approaching the Holland Tunnel. "I'm about to lose phone reception," I said. "Talk to you soon?" After another beat I said, "Wait, Jonas."

"Yes, Lily?"

"I miss you." The words came out without thought and it was too late to take it back I held my breath.

"I miss you, too. Talk to you soon." He hung up.

I thanked David as he walked back towards the elevators outside of my apartment. He had insisted on bringing up my new bags and backpack and seeing me inside the door. I indulged him as I now regarded him as a spy that would report my actions back to Jonas. I didn't know what to make of what Gregor and Jonas told me.

My phone chimed, alerting me of an incoming message. It was from Gregor.

I sincerely apologize for my inappropriate behavior. I'm sorry. I value you as my assistant and friend. I promise it will never happen again. Please accept my apology.

The knots in my stomach tightened. He was speaking weird. What did Jonas say to him?

You had me at apologize. It's fine. I'm ok. I know you didn't mean anything. I'll see you in the morning.

Take Monday off. You can make it a three day weekend.

I rolled my eyes at the phone.

I can't do that. You just got back from the conference. I'll be at work Monday.

I frowned. Was this some type of rivalry? Gregor suddenly kissing me and Jonas manipulating his business. Not sure. They both never promised me anything. So if I could manage to hold on, would I be able to hold him?

"Louis Vuitton?"

Natasha ran over from the couch and pulled the bag out of my hands and opened it. Inside she found, to my surprise, a matching handbag and a Paul McCartney and Wings and Double Fantasy CD. She quickly tossed the CDs to the side to stroke over the leather, springing to my mind imagery of Gollum in the Lord of the Rings.

I pick up the CDs and felt a flutter go through my chest. *He remembered.* "I have no idea," I said absently.

She pursed her lips. "I know you don't. So who is he?" Natasha asked.

I bit my bottom lip. "A friend."

She laughed. "Some friend. You were with him the

last few days. You could have told me." She sounded annoyed. She wheeled the bags and carried the handbag towards my bedroom and I followed after her.

"Would you mind if I borrow this one for Barbados? Ari is taking me there," Natasha said.

I hesitated. "Hum. Okay." I walked into my bedroom and put the CDs on the bed and started to unload my backpack for laundry when Natasha started speaking again.

"So, we're the same now," she said clasping her hands together.

I lifted my brows. "How so?"

"I have Ari and you have … what's his name?" she asked.

I busied myself with hanging my dress in the closet. Natasha continued speaking.

"It's better to tell him what you want next time. Not bad for your first."

I stopped and glared at her. "I don't know what you have going on with Ari, but Jonas isn't like that." I walk back to the bed and start unwrapping the CDs.

"Jonas who? Is he in the middle of a divorce?"

I flushed. "He was, but it's a friendship."

She flounced down on my bed. "Darling, so is Ari."

I gritted my teeth. What does she know? I didn't want to discuss Jonas with her. "Get out of my room."

"He sexed you for the last few days where? A hotel, I bet. He gives you expensive gift and controls your moving around. I'd say he's the same," she said.

I closed my eyes. I had become Natasha. Star Wars came to mind. My journey to the dark side was complete.

I narrowed my eyes. "Enough. I don't want to talk about Jonas with you."

"Why? Because you're in love with your sugar daddy," she snickered.

"Get the hell out of my room now." I motioned toward the door.

Natasha rose slowly. "Stop being dramatic. I'll borrow this bag, and you can borrow something for the next time. Go to Journelle or La Perla and get better lingerie. Ask. He'll take you there." She picked up the bag and walked to the door. "It's not so bad. My first lasted a good year. You just keep your eyes open for the next."

"When do you know to, uh, look?" I asked. Not that I would look, but I did need to be mindful of when I was getting replaced.

She smiled. "Smartest question you ever asked me. Less attentive. Cancels with you and starts talking about other female friends. He'll say 'friends,' but don't be stupid. She's your replacement."

I nodded. She closed the door behind her and I went and covered my face with my hands. Was this what I had in store for myself? A desire to maintain by hopping to the next wealthy man that took interest in me? Gregor even said I wasn't more than an occupation of his time. So how was I going to protect my heart?

I walked over to my CD player and put in Paul

McCartney and Wings *Maybe I'm Amazed*. I changed into my tank and shorts before doing sit-ups. After I finished, I walked to the bathroom and washed my face and brushed my teeth. Returning to my bedroom, I crawled inside my bed and inhaled deeply—I could still smell scent of Jonas's aftershave.

My heart squeezed as I recalled Jonas in my bed holding me. A few days ago? It seemed so much longer to me. After a while, I drifted then fell asleep.

The sound of my phone ringing woke me. I drowsily reached for my handbag and pulled it out. "Hello?"

"Hey."

I gritted my teeth. "Declan."

"Yes. Guess what I found?" he said.

I groaned. I hated when he played childish guessing games with me. "Just tell me."

"If you will change your attitude, I will," he grumbled.

I pushed my hair back. "I was sleeping."

"You're so lazy, Lily. It's barely eleven."

My eyes glazed over. *He's insulting me again.* "Okay. I'm going now."

"I was only joking with you. Damn you're sensitive and grumpy when you first wake up. Nothing's changed. Will you ever grow up?"

I sighed. *Except I don't care to listen to you talk about me.* "Did you have something you wanted to tell me?"

"I found a bunch of pictures of that last Perchance to Dream. It has pictures of you, me, your mom and dad, and all the kids. Remember we couldn't find them? Well I did, and more."

My pulse pounded in my chest. "More? What did you find Dec?"

"Say thank you and you're the best, and I'll tell you."

I puffed. "Thank you, you're the best."

"Not like that. The way you used to say it to me. Like you mean it."

"I'm sick." I lied. "Thank you for telling me, it means a lot to me. You're the best."

"That's my good girl. I miss you so much. I keep thinking about how you look now. I'd love to take you out. My friends are all asking about you."

I clenched my jaw. "I'm busy with work. So…."

"If you want the video, you'll go to lunch with me tomorrow."

I covered my mouth. "You have found the last video…?" I had searched for years for the video of me and my parents from the last year of our lives together, but never could find it. "Where did you find it?"

"Heather … I mean, I was cleaning out my place and found it. It's good. Even has the first dinner I came down to."

I pushed my hair back. "Thank you, Declan. But I won't be able to do lunch."

"But you want the video, don't you? You can't spare an hour after I found this for you? It's only a friendly lunch. Salomé's show courtesy and respect to everyone."

I stopped myself from the retort I wanted to say back

to him using my father's words to get his way. "Fine next Thursday. I have a lot of work to do and I won't be able to take more than an hour for lunch." I paused and pulled up my calendar. "How about between 12:00 and 1:00? I have a meeting at 1:15 with Gregor." *Well, I do now.*

He blew out and I knew he was smoking again. "Hmm. Okay. Good. I'll pick you up next Thursday. But I thought they were important to you."

My face fell. I didn't know how to answer that. So I said, "I thought you quit smoking?"

He chuckled. "See? You still care about me." Before I could respond, he hung up. I groaned in frustration. Why wouldn't he leave me alone? I thought bitterly. I heard more from him since I saw him at the hotel than when he broke up with me. Not to mention, he's engaged. Taking a deep breath, I sent a text message to Jonas.

Thank you for the CDs and the surprise addition of luggage. I don't know how this all works, but I would prefer no gifts. I hope you're over your jet lag. See you.

Before I could put it away, another call came in. "Declan?" I growled.

"No. Jonas," Jonas voice was curt. "You speaking with him?"

I bit my lip. "He called."

Jonas sighed. "I don't want you speaking with him."

I narrowed my brow. "He called to tell me he found photos and videos of my family."

"Okay. So he's sending them to you?" he asked.

His words hung in the air. I didn't want to upset him by telling him I agreed to go to lunch with Declan, but I also didn't want to lie. Why did I need to explain myself? *Unbelievable.*

"I'm sure he'll send them to me," I said quietly.

"Hmmm. Fair enough," he said. "Now, I got your message. What do you mean by 'how this works'?"

I closed my eyes. "It's late here and I have to run with Natasha tomorrow. Early."

"To hell with your run with Natasha. I want your answer."

I pursed my mouth. "I bet you wouldn't say that if it was something you had planned."

"You know what I meant. Stop playing games, or you'll face punishment the next time I'm in town."

"Punishment? For not answering? That's pretty heavy handed," I said.

"Lily, stop playing coy and tell me what's bothering you. Now," he ordered.

I exhaled. "Fine. My roommate Natasha explained how companionships work. I don't want gifts. I want this to be fifty-fifty."

"I don't have a nefarious plan in place for you. We'll discuss the latter when we see each other in ten days, maybe a week."

My lips parted. "A week?" my tone higher.

He chuckled. "That's better. Yes. I'm coming back. Hopefully for a few days or more."

"Yay!" I cheered and giggled. Shit. Should I have

done that?

"I want to see that beautiful smile and laugh. Get your laptop so we can Skype."

Dutifully, I went to my desk in the corner and pulled out my laptop and put it on the bed. I wanted so much to see him again. I connected to Skype and Jonas's gorgeous face filled the screen. He was still dressed in the black shirt from his morning. His hair slightly parted and hanging on the sides of his devastatingly handsome face. He was in what appeared to be an office with a large window displaying the bright skyline behind him.

"Please tell me you're not working," I said, annoyed.

His grin went lopsided. "No. I'm finished now. This is my office in my condo here," Jonas said. "You look sleepy and something else is going on. Tell me."

I sighed. "Well, Gregor mentioned I was a lot like Maggie."

Jonas mouth formed a line. "And from your expression, what he told you wasn't good."

I looked away. "Well. No, but I won't judge."

"Look at me," Jonas said and I turned to face the monitor again.

"I think I deserve to speak my side as you have heard Greg's. I mean Gregor's, as he now insists on being called," Jonas rolled his eyes. "Dani and I met him in college. We tried to get along with him, but he was ... well, we found him pretentious. Though in hindsight I'd call him ambitious. He name dropped, was pushy for introductions, connections ... that kind of thing," he paused.

I gave a slight nod. I loved Gregor like a good friend, but I knew Jonas's assessment about his ambition rang true. He continued. "One night we invited him to an event and he brought Maggie." He smiled wistfully. "Maggie was—"

"Like me?" I interrupted.

Jonas shook his head. "Not exactly. She had long dark hair and a curvy body, but no, she wasn't like you. She was, well…." Jonas grinned. "Uninhibited. We had a sexual friendship with her, but then Mag's was a free spirit, and we did enjoy our time together."

I looked away. I didn't really want the details of him with anyone, but I couldn't just end the conversation. So I asked what I really wanted to know, "Did you break it off with her?"

"Yes. She wanted to have more sexual partners, and that wasn't what we wanted. So it ended," Jonas said.

"How did she feel about it?" I asked.

"She was fine," Jonas said.

I licked my lips. "Did you see her after you broke up?"

"We didn't hang in the same social circles," he said with a slight lift of his shoulders.

I lowered my gaze. "You didn't talk to her anymore?"

Jonas gave me an odd look. "Yes. Not often, but we did. She was still our friend."

I stared at him through the screen. "Gregor cared for her a lot, it seems."

He nodded. "I know and she told us, but Maggie was only interested in sexual friendships. She liked Gregor and offered him an open relationship, but he refused, just as we did."

I lifted my brows. "So you didn't abandon her?"

He chuckled. "Hardly. But who knows what she told Gregor. She moved on. I saw her outside of college after that. Places Gregor wasn't privy or able to court invitations. We all mourned the end, but we parted mutually."

I exhaled and smiled. "Thanks. I wish you would tell Gregor that. He still has some feelings around what happened back then."

"Oh trust me, Gregor will be hearing from me," Jonas said curtly.

I chewed my lip. "Don't. Jonas. He just didn't understand."

"Poisoning your opinion of me will need to be answered for," he said, "but I don't want you to worry."

I frowned. "It was all a misunderstanding and I'm not poisoned, so please let it go."

"I don't want to talk about Gregor anymore," Jonas said. "Let me see you."

I pushed my hair in my face and we both laughed.

His sea blue eyes glimmered. "I want to see more than your hair. Take off your clothes."

My mouth dropped open at the swift change in our conversation. "Right now?"

He nodded. "Yes. Now."

I shook my head. "I don't think I can do that. It's

too embarrassing."

His silence was just as powerful as his command. The headiness of his attention pushed me past my insecurities. I found myself pulling off my top, and shorts. I then turned back to the screen in my black panties.

"All of it," he said in a low tone that sizzled through me.

Everything in my body swelled and tightened as I hooked my thumbs in the sides and pulled them off. He groaned in approval for me as he saw my naked body on the webcam. His eyes dark, as if devouring me.

"Are you wet? Show me." We both knew the answer, but I played along for him. I rested on my back and coated my fingers with my essence and held it up to the camera.

"I wish I was there to suck them. Do it for me." The carnal look he gave me made me hotter than I already was.

I placed my fingers in my mouth and sucked, tasting my own arousal.

He let out a grunt. "I'm envious. I wish I could bury my face there. Move the camera so I can see your sweet, hot pussy."

My skin was inflamed all over and his words made me ache for him. I moved the web camera exactly how he directed and the wicked smile that I saw on the screen let me know he was turned on by me.

"You're glistening for me. So beautiful. Know I want to be there. Know I can't wait to be inside you again."

I moaned. My need growing and longing for his touch. "Jonas. I want you."

"Touch yourself and show me," he demanded.

I stroked my fingers around my clit and dipped inside. Jonas's groans and moans pushed me along and the sight of his hunger edged me to continue to stroke myself, my ears filling with the slick sound of my sex as I pushed my fingers inside until I quivered in climax.

"Mmm. So. Beautiful. Lily," Jonas said. "Thank you."

I shivered and mumbled, "Sure."

He exhaled long. "You didn't want to share that with me?" he asked in an amused tone.

I sighed. "Yes, but now. It's awkward. Weird."

He chuckled. "Nothing weird, just a little erotic web play."

"I just want you to touch me," I whined.

"I know. I'll make it up to you when I see you. I promise," he said, his voice smooth as silk.

I nodded and he gave me one of his gorgeous smiles at the camera. "Smile for me." I beamed.

"Lovely. Good night, Lily."

"Good night, Jonas." I turned off the program and my laptop. What was I doing? How could I do that? It wasn't me, was it? Something about Jonas Crane's attention and demand had taken a hold of me. I was already seeking to please him. I was already looking forward to the next time I would see him.

Seducing me during our initial dinner had been easy.

He was captivating and engaging. His beauty and charm, as well as the easiness of our conversation, had hooked me. But then he asked me to be his companion, and I had agreed to try. A chance to go out and have sex with a gorgeous man seemed easy enough. But what I didn't know was that his companionship came with his apt attention to everything that I was and wanted to be. Indeed, the more I played over in my mind the precursor "his" to his companionship, the more pang I felt in my heart. And in there lurked the danger. I was and wanted to be his, but Jonas wasn't mine.

Jonas couldn't be accused of being passive when it came to me and our companionship. He had proven himself to be attentive in and out of bed, to the degree of overwhelming. Somehow, in only a short amount of time, he had established himself in all aspects of my life. His time, attention, sexual intimacy, and care, just not his commitment. I wasn't allowed to claim or keep him. Eventually, there was going to be an end. *So I just need to be careful. Too early to worry anyway.*

I walked out of my bedroom and into the bathroom, where I turned the shower on cold and cleaned myself. I brushed my teeth and moisturized my face. Drying off, I returned to my room and put my phone and laptop away, collapsing on the bed. After a while, I finally fell asleep.

CHAPTER SIXTEEN

THE WEEKEND FLEW by and so did the week. After Gregor's conference, Arch was inundated by submissions and press attention. Gregor was almost back to himself, though he still kept a professional distance. Before I knew it, Thursday rolled around and I was checking my email every few minutes to find out when Jonas would be returning to New York. On my fifth pass through my inbox, I found a letter from Ms. Hilda Parker. She was managing the Salomé's Love Legacy Art Week this year.

Dear Lily,

Everyone is very excited about the Salomé' Love Legacy.

Thank you for organizing the letters and sending them to the previous year's sponsors.

On a sad note, some have come back and said that due to financial cuts, they won't be able to contribute. We still have another six months, so perhaps it will pick up. Any ideas, please let me know.

Thank you so much,
Ms. Parker,
Marymount Elementary

I sulked. What was I going to do now? I knew I wouldn't be able to afford to sponsor the program on my own. I bit my lip and quickly forwarded her letter to the Dean of Students at Boston University to see if she would be willing to get the students involved in a phone campaign this year. I also forwarded it to Mary to ask if she knew someone at Boston Conservatory that may be able to connect with Ms. Parker to help out. I wasn't ready to let it go, and the only way I knew to cover the cost was to get the promotion from Arch. That involved Jonas.

Jonas Crane. He was becoming an obsession. My mind constantly replaying my time with him. Longing to see and feel him again. Constantly checking my phone and email, for anything to assure me that he was think-ing about me and wanted to be with me. I knew my thoughts were dangerous, as he was quite clear in his expectation of me. He wanted me on his terms as his companion available to do and go wherever he wanted when he came back to New York City.

My phone beeped. I looked down and groaned as I realized it was a text from Declan.

How about Bryant Park Grill for lunch?

My stomach churned. I had agreed to meet him for lunch on Thursday, but everything inside me said to not go. However, I reminded myself that he had photos and video of my parents. The photos I was convinced were ruined in the accident, but he said he had them. I needed to be his "good girl" in order for him to give them to me.

How about Sergio's? I need to be back at 1:00 on the dot.

He replied. *Yeah. Okay. See you at 12:00. Can't wait.*

I narrowed my eyes, but turned on my computer. I didn't like Declan treating this like a date, but I didn't mention it because I wasn't sure of his response. My mind chimed in, *if you're not sure, you shouldn't go.* But there was no way I would cancel. He had remembered the years I looked for them and was thoughtful enough to bring them to me. *Maybe we can be friends. Like Jonas and Dani.*

I stood up and walked over to Gregor's office and peered in. He was bent over typing at his computer. "Hey."

"Hello, Lily. I'm on with Brodsky in a few minutes," Gregor said without stopping. "Is there something you need help with?"

I chewed my lip "No. I have … Well, Declan found some photos and videos and I was going to go to get them from him at noon, unless you need me?"

His head shook as he stayed on task. "No. I won't. Thank you."

I folded my arms. "Gregor, come on. Let it go." I started singing the chorus from the movie Frozen. His shoulders shook a little, which let me know he amused; however, he still wouldn't turn around.

I hunched my shoulders. "Okay. I'll be at my desk,"

I mumbled.

What did Jonas say to him? Was it because of the kiss? I worked steadily as Gregor continued to avoid me communicating through emails and the phone. My worry about our working relationship had preoccupied my mind so much so that when Declan called and I noticed it was ten after 12:00. I had to run out of the building to meet him.

"About time you came out. I work in the village, or have you forgotten," Declan griped as I climbed inside his range rover.

"I'm sorry, Dec. I told you I had work—" I stammered.

"But you couldn't choose a place in between midtown and the village for lunch. You know I work in the village and this is at least a twenty-minute drive in lunch traffic," Declan scowled at me. "So spoiled."

I dropped my head. I didn't want to point out that he had chosen Bryant Park, which was even further away, just this morning. "How about we go wherever you want to go?" I offered.

Declan grunted and started driving. "I don't have much time, so yeah. We'll have to eat at Parco's." Parco's was a small chain sandwich shop a few doors down from his work, and would take me an extra half hour just to return to work by subway. I wanted to protest; but he had something I wanted and the best way to get it was to be accommodating. "Okay."

"Good girl," Declan said. His lips curled into a smug

grin. He turned on talk radio and laughed along with it all the way through downtown and the village.

Once we reached Bleecker Street, he parked his car in his regular parking space. He turned and assessed me. "You look *okay*. You want to go inside and say hello to everyone? They always ask about you."

I looked down at my watch. "We don't have much time and I really will be late getting back to work." My pulse sped up as he went still next to me.

"A princess can't spare a few minutes," he said venomously. "You want to just run off after I went through the trouble of picking you up—"

"No. I want to have lunch," I stammered interrupting him.

Declan snickered, "Yeah, you want to eat. Always ready to stuff your face. Of course."

My face fell as a lump formed in my throat. "I'm not all that hungry. I can come in and say hello."

"I was just joking." He chuckled. Suddenly he grabbed my hair bun and yanked my head back, exposing my neck. "Stop acting funny and talking weird to me," he said.

As I took in ragged breaths, my hands reached up to my neck to soothe the pain there. *He hasn't hit me. He's just frustrated,* I lulled myself.

"Let go, Dec," I gritted, trying to remain calm. He let go with force enough to slam my forehead against the dashboard.

I cried out and clutched my head. "Ouch. What are

you doing? You asshole!"

"What the fuck did you call me?" Declan gripped my head and banged it against the dashboard again.

I clawed into him. "Stop." He took both of his hands and with added force pushed my head against the dash again. Sinking my nails into his hands and arms, my voice rose louder. "Wake-up. Stop it." Another, this time with more strength. He was gone, and nothing registered. I clawed into him as hard as I could, letting out a high-pitched scream.

"Fuck that hurt!" he yelped. "Why are you screaming?"

Good. I hope it hurts. My breath came in and out fast as I tried to still my rapid pulse. My mind raced as it struggled through Declan's attack.

I covered my face with my hands. I grabbed the door, but found it locked.

"Shit. I didn't mean to do that," Declan said. "Wait, please don't leave. You're too delicate. I forgot I can't *horseplay* with you."

I frantically looked around outside and saw no one was around. No one had witnessed it. "Don't touch me. I'm leaving."

"Please don't go," Declan pleaded. "Don't leave me like everyone else." He dropped his head. "It's been hard for me. I lose contracts at work. I barely get time off. I've got nobody. Nobody," he said mournfully. He glanced up at me. "You look like your mom. She was so pretty. She was so good to me, I loved her like she was mine. I guess she kind of was, after my foster mom died. I think about her every day, probably why it was hard to be with you, because I see her in you … you know. I miss her."

My heart felt heavy in my chest as I listened to him and assessed my injuries. My face throbbed in pain. I felt a scrape along my scalp that was damp.

"I miss her, too," I mumbled.

"You're the only one that gets me. Please. It was an accident. I was looking forward to seeing you and giving you the video and pictures."

My throat closed and I stared down at my hands, unable to speak.

"Look at us. Only passion causes this much feeling," he said. "We have passion between us. I knew we'd always end up together. We deserve each other." He reached over and tried to pull me into a hug.

I cringed and moved as far away as I could manage in the seat. "Don't touch me."

Declan frowned. "You're acting dramatic. Trying to drag this out. You're alright. You don't look bad. I said I'm sorry. Just give me a few minutes before you head back. Please, Lily? We still got things to talk about, right?"

My face throbbed in pain. *Yeah my video and photos. My memories.* "I can only stay a few minutes."

"Hmm, yeah right." Declan sat back and gave me a steely stare. "Go in Parco's and get yourself together. I'll order a salad and soup for you."

I quickly exited his car and headed into Parco's.

Once through the door, I kept my eyes on the beige parquet flooring and made a beeline for the bathroom that was around the small island counter in the back. When I stood before the small porcelain sink, and looked into the small mirror, I shook. *What did I do that set him off?*

"Horseplay," I muttered.

My mind journeyed back to the first time I heard those words from him.

2:38 a.m. I knew the time as I was staring at the black and grey clock on the side table in Declan's apartment in Chelsea. I reached my hand back to feel the opposite side of the bed. Cool to the touch.

Where's Dec? I grouched as I threw the sheets off and stumbled to the door. I wiped my eyes and reached out for the handle, jerking it open. The sound of snoring filtered across my ears. He was on the couch. I stomped down the hall to his small living room and found him stretched out on his leather couch. Still dressed in the jeans and shirt he had on when he left for a short visit a few hours ago. The stench of alcohol permeated his pores, causing bile to rise in my throat. He had promised he wouldn't drink. I pursed my lips as I reached out and pushed hard against his shoulder. "Dec. You're drunk again," I announced the obvious. His lids fluttered open on the third pass.

"Oh for fuck sake. Go to bed, Lily," he said, closing his eyes again.

"No," I yelled. "I'm going back to Boston." I turned and slowly started moving towards his bedroom.

"Wait," he called out.

I picked up my pace and jogged back to the bedroom. I could hear Dec on my heels as I ran inside and grabbed my trolley bag.

"Lily. Stop," Dec said. *He reached over and tugged on my bag.*

"No. I'm leaving," I said, snatching the bag out of his grip. He grabbed the bag and we tugged between us. I let go and he stumbled back, hitting the back of his dresser and shaking all the bottles lined on top of it. His face scrunched. I stopped, wondering if he was hurt. He gripped my bag and twisted it, breaking the seal and threw it on the floor.

"What the hell are you doing? You ass—" Dec grabbed my shoulders and shook me. *"Let go,"* I yelled. He didn't answer. Just stared as his hands gripped tighter.

"Stop," I shouted, feeling somewhat frightened.

He shoved me hard and I fell backwards, my head connecting with the corner of his oak dresser. "Oww." I cried out, my hands moving to soothe the pain on my head.

"Shit. Lily," Dec said. *"Let me see."* He bent down.

I inched away, my eyes widening and my mouth dropping open. "Stay away from me. You...." I stared at him in disbelief. I couldn't say the words. Dec had hit me.

"No. We were both horseplaying, and you hit that by accident." He started crying. *"I didn't hit you. I love you. Please don't leave me,"* his voice was so small. I reached out and wrapped my arms around his neck to comfort him. Horseplaying.

It wasn't horseplay that time or this time. But I was too scared. Too stupid, I scolded myself. He didn't hurt me again for almost a year after that. And I stayed because I didn't want to leave him alone. He needed me and I needed him. But not anymore. I needed to go.

Oh. how I wanted to go! But what about my photos and videos? The last days with my parents. The last records of those moments of us together as a family. My eyes misted as a vice clamped around my heart. The last video. My father insisting on creating it and I had no idea that would be the last recording of our time together as a family. Thinking of that video made me feel like a little girl longing for her mommy and daddy. I wanted to see and experience our time as a family again where we loved and cherished each other. The time before I was alone. An orphan with no one. That last kiss, that last hug. Surely I had gone through too much to just walk away empty handed. I had to get myself together and go back out there and get Declan to give the videos and photos to me.

I swallowed hard. *Heaven knows what my father would think of me right now.* Averting my reflection in the mirror, I washed the wound and pulled my hair down and styled it, but wasn't able to cover the swelling or the bruise. I searched my handbag and cursed myself, realizing I didn't have any makeup to cover it. I tried applying a cold-water compress to it and sighed. I had no more time and I needed to get through the rest of lunch and leave the deli. I pulled out three pain pills and cupped water in my hand to take them, then walked out of the bathroom.

I walked back to the front of Parco's. Declan waved me over to the plastic table where he was seated. He held up a salad in a plastic container.

"You were in there long enough," Declan joked as he bit into his sandwich.

I plastered a smile as I uncovered the salad container. *He forgot the soup?* I wouldn't ask. I sipped the cup of water on the table. "How much was my salad?"

He rolled his eyes at me. "I invited you to lunch. It's my treat."

"Thanks." I started eating the salad as Declan talked about his work, friends, and travel. Interjecting at all places appropriate as I tried to stop the churning of my stomach.

I swallowed hard as I eyed the clock at the counter. "It's 1:15 p.m. I need to leave. So, Dec, can I see the pictures?"

He went still across from me.

"I'm so excited to see them," I added.

He widened his eyes and covered his mouth. "Oh shit. I forgot them at home. I'm so sorry."

My eyes filled and I turned my head, putting my handbag on my shoulder. *Did he ever really have them?* I doubted it. "I need to get going. Thanks for lunch."

"I could bring them by your house later," Declan said, his gaze flicking over me.

I screamed inside, but shook my head and he squinted. "No. Maybe it would be better if I don't see them. I think the videos and photos will probably just upset me," I lied, my only defense hoping to curb his satisfaction in my disappointment.

He studied me, then nodded. "Well, I'll hold onto them until you feel you're ready."

I bit my lip hard and stood. "Sure," I muttered bitterly.

Declan frowned but stood. "I love you, Tiger Lily."

I flinched as he leaned in and I turned away before his mouth made contact with my lips. Dipping my head to hide my scowl, I walked briskly out of the deli.

Who was that Declan? I didn't know what I did to make him want to hurt me. I waved my hands frantically and managed to flag down a taxi. While I wanted to try to make sense of what happened, I knew what I needed right now was to be away from him. His lies. His cruelty.

Breathe, I told myself as I sat in the back of the taxi and it sped off down the road. I folded my arms around myself. My mind started to race. Did he do that to hurt me? Why did he enjoy hurting me? My phone buzzed.

A call from a number I didn't recognize. I hesitated. Would Declan go through the trouble of borrowing a phone? I didn't know. Still, I took a deep breath. The residue of his violence covered me, and bile rose in my throat. My heart pounded as the phone continued to chime. I could always hang-up, I thought.

I cleared my throat and answered, "Hello?"

"Hello, Lily. This is Fiona from Barneys New York. How are you today?" she asked.

I released my breath. "Hello? Sorry. I didn't order anything from Barneys. I think you have the wrong number."

"Well, I was informed to contact you by Mr. Crane. Are you familiar with him?"

I sat up straighter. "Yes. I know Mr. Crane. What is this about, Fiona?"

"I'm calling to set an appointment for you to meet with me for a new wardrobe. If you could make it today or tomorrow after 4:00 that would work best. Now I'll need your size—"

New wardrobe? "Excuse me," I said interrupting her.

I pinched the bridge of my nose and winced, having forgot the tenderness there. My nerves jittered as I thought on Gregor's story of Jonas seducing Maggie with expensive gifts. Pulling her into a lifestyle she wasn't able to maintain when he left her. This seemed to be Jonas's modus operandi, his usual way he treated his companions. My stomach churned. I didn't want to be thought of as or treated as any of his other women.

"Mr. Crane never mentioned this to me. I'd need to speak with him."

"I understand. But could you perhaps make the appointment now and then speak with him?"

I licked my lips. "I apologize, but I'll need to speak with him. First."

"Okay. Please call me back ASAP if you can though. I'm usually booked, but I was asked to set an emergency appointment for you." She said her tone light.

"I'll try to speak with him right now," I said thanking her and hung up. I shook as I pressed Jonas's number. After a couple of rings he answered.

"I called your desk at work, but you were out. I tried your cell but it went to voicemail," he began.

My tension eased a bit. He tried to reach me. "I didn't receive a message. I had an appointment outside of work. I'm on my way back there now." My stomach lurched. I didn't like lying, but I knew I wouldn't tell him what happened with Declan. I hadn't thought it all out myself. Partially out of pride, and fear of what he would or wouldn't do to him.

"Have you been crying?" his voice softened.

My heart contracted. How did he know? Nothing seemed to get past him. Biting my lip, "I'm alright. I might be getting a cold."

He exhaled into the phone. "Hmm. When David picks you up tonight, I'll have him pick up some soup and some of Dani's special cold remedy tea."

I closed my eyes against the concern I heard in his voice. My mother was right, one lie always leads to another. "I'm really okay. Please don't do that," I said quietly. My eyes dilated. "Wait. Why is David picking me up and why is Fiona from Barneys calling me?"

"David escorts my son Paul and he will take you wherever you need to go too, and before you protest, you're alone in New York. It'll keep you safe. So that's non-negotiable," he said with authority. "As for shopping, I have a few events coming up and as my companion, you will need clothing to wear to attend them."

I pressed my lips together. He had thought of everything without even talking to me. This type of heavy handiness was starting to bother me. "I can get things on my own. Just tell me what's coming up."

"I've been invited to a state dinner, charity auction, and a conference. I won't attend all," Jonas said. "But I'd need you to be ready. These are public events, press events."

Gregor was right. I was over my head and out of my league. I didn't have anything that would fit the events listed, or the fashion knowledge to dress for them, but I still didn't want to accept his gifts.

"Oh, perhaps, I could attend one of those," I stuttered.

"No," Jonas said. "If I'm attending them then I expect you to attend as well."

Was it all or nothing? Would he get someone else? I couldn't refrain from asking. "Wouldn't it be easier to just go out with someone that has all of this already?" I said barely above a whisper.

"Is that what you want?" Jonas asked, his voice just as soft.

I tucked my hair back. "No. I don't. I want to go with you. But I don't want you buying me…."

"I'm not buying you," Jonas said, his tone sharp. He exhaled into the phone. "It's for my own selfish reasons I'm getting them for you. There's no need to protest."

I looked out the window and stared at the people along the sidewalks as he stopped and started through the streets back uptown. We were a few blocks from the office. "A dress. Nothing more. I'll take it as a loan until I get my raise or promotion," I said sucking in air.

"Did Gregor promise a raise and a promotion?" Jonas asked, his tone sardonic.

I chewed my lip. "No. He didn't. I'm just hoping." I sighed in exasperation. "Leave him alone, Jonas, please. Let it go," I said in a rush.

"I could get you a new job anywhere you want paying three times what you make for less hours," he offered.

I pressed my lips together. "Is it that easy for you? No. Thank you."

"Why won't you let me help you?" Jonas asked, his voice raised in frustration.

I groaned. "Why are you trying to change me? I wish you wouldn't treat me this way. My situation is different, but I didn't set out to take advantage or…."

"I'm not trying to change you," Jonas said in an exasperated tone. "I don't feel taken advantage of and I want to help you. I understand that this is overwhelming, but I knew that you'd need things for some of the events when I asked you to spend time with me. But I won't waiver on my expectations though. That extends to your clothing."

"Well, if you put it that way," my voice was thick.

"Don't get upset. It really is nothing," he said. "I

don't usually have to fight to help, or even over little gifts and a ride home. This is new to me."

How many times had he done this before? I wanted to ask, but I didn't. I didn't want to imagine Jonas doing anything he did with me with someone else.

I sighed. "This is new to me too."

"I haven't received the information on the Legacy. Send it when you get to the office," he ordered.

"I don't want you to…." I sighed. Could I put my pride before the children? I wouldn't. It was all too much. Jonas was too much. "You're so bossy. I feel like I'm at work instead of…."

"Instead of what?" His voice softening.

"Instead of chatting. I don't know. Lightly conversing with…." I let the words go unsaid. *With the man I like a lot.*

"I would have been open to light if you weren't fighting with me," Jonas said.

The taxicab stopped and I reached inside my purse to pay the driver "I'll do what you want, just leave my boss and job alone," I said in finality.

"I know you will do what I want," Jonas said, his tone low.

My body heated up just from his words and tone. "Jonas. We're not talking about that," I said huskily.

"About what?" Jonas asked.

"I can't right now," I ran through the doors of the Arch building, "I'm at work."

"You could. But you'll do that and more when I see

you," he said. "I'll have Dani check in with you on the weekend for me."

"No. That's not necessary. I've got work to catch up on." I waved to Olivia in reception, her jaw dropped open.

"Lily what happened to your face," Olivia said loud-ly.

"What did she say?" Jonas asked.

I shook my head at Olivia. "Nothing. I can't wait to see you again." I covered my mouth.

I could hear the crackles of Jonas exhaling into the phone. "Answer David's call. I'll speak with you later." He hung up.

I cursed. I shouldn't have said that to him. I didn't understand why I couldn't stop myself from saying words that exposed my feelings for him. I was going to lose him. But could I lose what I didn't have?

"Lily, what happened to your face?" Olivia called out again moving my attention away from my thoughts and back to her gaping mouth, which shut closed as my eyes made contact with hers.

My hands trembled as I tried to cover my face. "I fell on the concrete and hit my head."

Olivia was a retired cop. There was something about the way she stared at me that had pinned me to the spot. I took an inventory of myself as she seemingly assessed me. My injury was concentrated along my temple and partial on left side of my face. My hands had no marks or scrapes. My clothing, no dirt or distress, nylons had no rips or shifts at the knee, and shoes polished, leather, nothing. Her eyes settled back on me again, this time hooded, meeting mine, which were watery.

My bottom lip trembled. Had she unmasked me?

"Did you need something, Lily?" Olivia asked, her tone reserved for children.

I dropped my gaze. I needed a hug. Some reassurance. Care. Love.

"No. Thanks, Olivia." I walked past her station. "I'm fine."

CHAPTER SEVENTEEN

I TOOK THE stairs to avoid running into anyone else at work. Once I reached my floor, I stopped at Gregor's office and hesitated. If Olivia noticed, so would he. And there was no telling what he would do. I needed to leave before that happened. I just needed time to decide what I was going to do, on my own.

Nothing. You never do anything. And you never will.

I walked over to my work cube and sent him a message.

"Would you mind if I worked from home the remainder of the day? I can email the documents I'm working on from there."

After a few minutes he messaged me back.

"Great idea. See you Monday."

My phone beeped. *David.* I pressed ignore and called the car service and packed up everything to take with me and went downstairs. My phone went off again. This time, I answered "Yes?"

"It's Dani. Jonas said you might be sick?"

"It's nothing. I'm fine. On my way home," I stammered.

"I want to come pick you up," Dani said.

"No," I said, raising my voice. "Sorry, no. The car service is here to pick me up. Thanks."

"I can come over for a visit. I won't hold you up too long," she said.

"Just … please. I'm fine," I said quietly. "I'm sorry, Dani, for being rude. But I must go."

"Okay, Lily. I'll respect that," Dani said. "But I'll still send David to drop some things off to you over the weekend." Keeping my head down, I left the office and headed for the subway home.

My phone beeped on the way and I took it out to check the messages. One missed call from David, and three texts from Declan.

Today was a wake-up call. I signed up for Anger Management classes like you asked me to, remember? I wasn't always like this, you know. I need help so thank you for helping me. The rent went up on my shop. I can't afford to miss work. If I do, I'll lose everything.

I erased the messages and blocked his phone number. I sighed in relief, though. At least he was going for help.

Arriving at my apartment, I caught a glimpse of Natasha climbing into Ari's Maserati and realized with glee she would be away at least until Monday. I would have the apartment all to myself.

Pondering their relationship, I absently went inside the building. They had been together at least four months, but she didn't believe it would go over a year. All that time they shared, gone?

In almost two weeks of knowing Jonas, I was already feeling for him something more than I ever felt for Declan. I didn't know how I could possibly handle months and not want or need more, and how would he handle it if I did? Would I have to hide my feelings, or would he have to break up with me?

Taking the elevator up to my apartment, I didn't know what I was to do. But I didn't have the time to think about it. I still had work hours to make up.

My stomach grumbled as I walked inside, prompting me to immediately go to the refrigerator and eat two of Natasha's fat free strawberry yogurts. I went to the bathroom and took a couple more pain pills to alleviate the pain. Declan. I let him in and he hurt me. He hadn't hit me in thirteen months. *Why?* I asked myself as I took a shower, but no reason came to mind.

Changing into my favorite black tank and shorts, I returned to the living room and set up a makeshift workstation on my couch with my laptop. By 8:00 that evening, I had managed to clear my inbox and send all of my work deliverables to Gregor.

Surfing through the channels on TV, I found a Star Trek marathon on the SyFy channel and grabbed my phone to check it before settling in. My heart sunk. One text message from David regarding a care basket from Dani. But David wasn't who I wanted to hear from. I wanted Jonas. I decided to call Mary to alert her to the marathon and ask for some advice.

"Updates, please," Mary ordered as soon as she

picked up.

I closed my eyes. "I went to see Declan, only because he said he had the missing photos from the art week. But then he said he forgot them at lunch, and ... Well, it didn't go well. I don't think he ever had them at all. Gregor kissed me. And Jonas is pressuring me with gifts, but no real promises of anything more. I like him so much, though. I don't know."

"Firstly, let's start with the easiest. I agree. Declan doesn't have the photos or videos. If he does, he's the scummiest scumbag in all of scumville," she said venomously. "He won't leave it at that. How did you leave it?"

The bite in her tone had my stomach in knots. Mary truly hated Declan and I hated myself for lying. But I didn't want her to know he hurt me, too. That would only make this worse. "I know now, but I had to find out." I cleared my throat. "So what should I do about Gregor?"

"Well, even if he likes you, he's definitely put off by your Jonas. Just act like nothing happened. He would want that now," Mary said.

I rubbed my chest. "Jonas isn't 'my Jonas,'" I said, stretching my legs out on the couch. "I'm just his companion."

"You like him a lot already, I can tell," she said.

I sighed. "Yes. I do."

"That's what I'm worried about." Mary sighed. "He's clear on what he wants from you. So there won't be more than that from him. You can and will get hurt if you're getting attached. Maybe you should end it."

I shut my eyes. "I don't want to end it, Mary."

"Just give it some thought, please?" she said. "As far as the clothing. It goes hand in hand with the agreement. If you are bumping shoulders with socialites, you can't wear cheap threads. You'll stand out, and not in a good way."

I looked at the ceiling. "That makes me feel a little better."

"I want you to feel better, but I have some bad news. I could only get five students to help with the phone-a-thon for the Love Legacy this year. So if you could add more funds to get students to sign-up to do a phone-a-thon., I can spread the word around campus?" Mary asked.

"If I get a raise or promotion, I could. But I'm not sure about that now," I said sadly. "I still have to pay my own pledge this year."

"Maybe Jonas could help you? I know that might muddy the waters more, but," she hesitated.

I paced. "Yeah, he already offered. I mean, he actually demanded to help me."

"Let him. You'll work it all out. 'Salomé's meet challenges head on,'" Mary said in a mockingly deep voice like my fathers.

I groaned. "Not funny, Mary. But thanks. I'm … I'm listening."

"I'm always here whatever you decide, my beautiful kept friend." She hung up.

Flopping back down on the couch, my mind went over all that happened, and where I stood with Jonas Crane. After ignoring everyone about Declan, it wasn't as easy to sweep my worries away.

The thought of not seeing Jonas ached my chest. But Mary and Gregor were right. This wasn't me and forming an attachment to a man set on not getting attached was a sure path to a heartache. Searching my heart, I feared too late. Jonas was under my skin, and I wasn't one to let go easy.

Dozing in front of the TV after five back-to-back episodes of Star Trek Next Generation, my text message alert went off. Jonas.

How are you feeling?

Awful. I swallowed hard. *Better thanks.*

Get plenty of rest. Bad news. Plans changed. I have to go to San Francisco.

My stomach flipped. *So you won't be able to come back to New York?*

He texted back: *No. Sorry.*

I frowned. *I'm disappointed. I'll miss you. I wish you could change it.* I typed, then erased it. Instead, I texted back:

I understand. I hope you can come back before you go back to Texas.

His response came almost immediately. *I want you to fly to San Francisco and join me.*

My eyes lit up. Jonas wanted to spend time with me during his work conference. Of course I knew I was making more of it than it was, but I still found it encouraging. I replied. *Really? Yes!!*

I would have to get approval from Gregor, I didn't think it would be a problem, though.

He replied. *Did that put a smile on your face?*

I giggled and texted back. *Yes it did :)*

He responded: *I wish I could see it, but I'm at a show with a friend.*

My brows puckered. *Girl or boy?* I wanted to ask, but didn't.

I'm curled up on the couch watching Star Trek.

He texted back. *If you added naked, I'd abandon my seat to see you on webcam.*

I felt a laugh escape from somewhere deep inside. *You pervert. I'm not doing that again!*

We both know you will do that and more if I tell you to.

My face warmed up as a tremor went through me. Jonas was right. Submitting to his demands thrilled me. *When you are here.*

He responded: *Every night before you sleep, I want you to masturbate. Think of my hands on you. But on Wednesday night, you're not allowed to come. I'll take care of you on Thursday.*

Heat flooded my body as I read his text. With images of doing his command. How would he know if I did it? He must have read my mind, because he texted

I'll know the second I see you. You could test me, but you might not like your punishment. Think last time, but more. You tied down.

I thought about how he had denied me an orgasm after the opera and frowned. *No thanks.*

To the tying down too?

I licked my lips and sent back. *Not sure.* And I wasn't.

Good. Talk to you soon. Tiger.

A pang went through my chest as I read the name. Tiger. Shortening it hurts less, though tiger by itself sure didn't describe how we were together.

More like a kitten with you. Talk to you soon. Miss you.

He wrote back. *My little tiger. We'll webcam this weekend. Get some rest.*

My heart squeezed. His tiger. Did he really think I belonged to him? Well as his companion, I did. In more ways than that if I had my way. If I could assert my will, but why push a man that doesn't want what you want? Mary was right. If he knew the truth I'd lose him. I'm losing him with every conversation, every share, and every dose of his company.

I touched my face and winced. Tracing with my fingertips the puffiness on my forehead. The lie hung in the air and around my neck like a noose.

Weak and stupid. No. I wouldn't allow Dec to hit me or even speak to him again.

More Lies. You're Declan's girl. Forever and always.

I didn't want to think about that. I had five days before seeing Jonas. Perhaps I could delay and see him later. Give me more time to heal my face and cover my heart. So I could continue lying? "Lies only lead to more lies. Before you know it, you've lost yourself in lies," my father taught me and he was right. Still I became a liar to them and everyone. All for a man that I used to love and couldn't hate.

My stomach soured as my conscience continued to badger me. When would the lies end? Would I be able to face everyone when they do? Would I be alone? Fear shot through me and I fought back to avoid it consuming me. *I can't deal with this right now.* I turned up the volume on the TV to drown out my thoughts and gave myself to the adventure before me.

CHAPTER EIGHTEEN

M Y HEADACHE WOKE me Saturday morning. Sharp stabbing pains. I touched my forehead. Swollen, throbbing sharp stabs of agony. Memories flooded my vision and I went dizzy. Declan grabbing my head and my clawing him like a cat to stop him. Bile rose in my throat.

Crawling out of bed, I opened my bedroom door and crossed the hall, making it in time to dry heave over the basin of the toilet. I rinsed my mouth and brushed my teeth, all the while avoiding my reflection and headache that pounded against my cranium. Putting off the inevitable wasn't working. I eyed the cabinet and pulled out the painkillers, taking three. I sighed and finally met my new enemy, the mirror. The truth of it all right there before me.

Yellow and purples decorated my forehead, the side of my face, and around my left eye. The evidence of Declan's attack still there. *The last time he hit me, it wasn't this bad.* The door chimed.

"Lily!" Natasha yelled. She was extra cranky because

Ari cancelled their weekend plans.

"Who's there?" I called out, my hand automatically seeking to cover my bruises. My heart pounded hard in my chest. I remained fixed, awaiting her response. After a few moments, she responded.

"No one. You have a delivery."

Pushing my hair in my face, I walked out of the bathroom and into the living area, where I found Natasha pawing through the basket.

"Dean and DeLuca basket. Good taste," Natasha said, a smile on her lips. "The note said Dani and Jonas." She motioned to the note on the table. I took a look at it.

Get better soon. Hugs. Dani and Jonas.

I chewed my lip as my stomach turned over. I lied to them. Looking at the bouquet of Tiger Lilies in the glass vase, I frowned. They even went as far as to send me flowers. I noticed a card and opened it. A letter and pictures. My face fell. Declan.

I couldn't reach you by phone to tell you but I'm checking into rehab today so you won't be able to reach me. I do love you Lily, but I need to sort myself out. Please forgive me. I didn't lie, here are some of the photos, but I know you want me to hold on to the rest.

Love Declan.

My vision clouded as I pulled out the pictures from the envelope. He hadn't lied after all. He had photos.

They weren't the photos from *Perchance to Dream*, but these were from a Sunday dinner at our Franklin street house in Quincy. My mind recalled taking a couple of photos of Declan with my parents, then us switching so he could take a couple of me with them.

Looking at them, I could see they were smiling in the photo with him, but not with their hearts. The pictures with me were brimming with love. They loved and cherished me, and I them. I had wanted to share that love of family with him. My heart ached. *Poor Dec.*

"Shit. What happened to your face?" Natasha said between bites of a pastry.

I grimaced. My anger at Declan's attack flared to life again. Not poor Declan. He hurt me. "I fell." I gestured toward the basket. "You could have asked before eating."

"Like you did with my yogurt?" Natasha said, pursing her lips.

I shrugged, but she was right. "Okay. We're even."

"You won't eat carbs anyway. Better not to waste them," Natasha said as she polished off the pastry. "Running tomorrow?"

"I might have to go to Barneys tomorrow," I said.

Natasha facial expression reminded me of winners of the lottery. "Oh. This is serious. But you need help. I'll go with you."

I bit my lip. I already didn't want to go, but with Natasha it would be just that much more difficult. "I have a shopper."

She rolled her eyes. "Stop being silly. This is the one

thing I can help you with. You traveling?"

My mouth turned down. I leaned on the counter and rested my head on my hand. "Yeah. San Francisco."

"Did he send an agenda?" she asked crossing her arms.

I shook my head. "No."

She rolled her eyes. "Well then, he will have to pay for that mistake."

I scrunched my face and winced. "Oh no, he will not. I was only getting a dress."

"Forget it," she said, glaring at me as she grabbed another pastry. "Do something about your face. I might have some cream that could help. I'll leave it on your bed."

I sighed. "If I go, you can come with."

Collecting the photos I returned to my room and picked up my phone.

I wanted to send a text to Dani, thanking her for the basket.

Thank you. I'm feeling better.

I wiped my face and erased the message. *Lying. I keep lying.* My body shook as I typed out a new reply.

I'm not sick. I hit my head. Sorry. I didn't want Jonas to worry. Thank you for the beautiful basket. I pressed send. Still lying. My phone buzzed.

"Lily, you fell? You're hurt?" Dani asked.

I closed my eyes, the back of my throat aching. "Uh. Yeah."

"I'll come over. Maybe you should get checked out by the doctor," Dani said.

I swallowed hard. "No. Please. I'm fine."

"You don't sound fine," Dani said.

Tears squeezed out of the corner of my eye. "I am. I just fell. I didn't want Jonas to worry. And I was … I am … embarrassed. I'll be fine. So, thank you for the basket. I must go now. Thanks again." I ended the call.

Staring down at the phone, I realized Declan was still hurting me. Every lie felt like another hit. I knew I should report this. Yet I was willing to help him instead. Every lie ate away at me. I'd been lying for years. I didn't even think. After all, he was getting help. *I can't interrupt that.* I didn't want to destroy his life. Did he care he was destroying mine?

I rubbed my empty stomach. I should eat, but I didn't have an appetite.

Telling Dani something close to the truth left a window for Jonas. This need for comfort and care was making me risk everything. And it was dangerous. In truth, I wanted and needed Jonas more than he wanted me. He didn't set out to hurt me. Still, I was hurting.

My phone buzzed and my heart and thoughts raced. *Jonas.* Pain seared my chest There couldn't be San Francisco or anymore with him. There was no time left and I knew what I needed to do. What I'd have to do.

"You fell? Get on the webcam," he said the second I answered.

I swallowed hard. "I can't."

"You mean you won't," his tone sharp. "Dani said you fell. You never mentioned anything to me yesterday.

Now tell me the truth."

I shut my eyes tight. "I am telling the truth. You say you want a companion, but you act like there's more. It feels like more. And I can't do it anymore."

"Get on the cam, Lily. Let's talk about this." Jonas exhaled. "Please," he added.

My heart ached at the anguish in his voice. "I can't anymore. I just I can't do this with you. Please understand. I feel like I want more. I'm getting attached to you. And you said you didn't want that," my voice faltered.

"You're doing this over the phone?" he said in frustration. "Let's talk this out. We can discuss this."

I sobbed, "It won't change my feelings. I can't do this anymore. It's hurting me. I can't handle this companionship. I can't be your companion anymore. Please understand." The only sound was my pulse pounding in my ears. My hand gripped the phone tightly as tears poured down my face. Jonas had said he didn't want a relationship, and I hadn't left much room for negotiation. After a few more minutes, he finally spoke.

"I'm still here. Anything you need. I still want to know about you, Tiger Lily," Jonas said his voice graveled.

I gulped. My heart shattering inside me. "I. I...." I sucked in air. "I. I just can't right now," I whispered and hung up.

I threw my phone, at the moment, I didn't care if it ever worked again.

I didn't hear it shatter and the thought arose, *he could call again.* But that wasn't going to happen. There wasn't a reprieve to hide away from the sorrow now gripping me. So I crawled under the covers, I curled myself in a ball, and cried. I cried for the photos and video of my parents I'd never get to see. I cried for the physical and mental attack by Declan.

I cried for Gregor's friendship. For not being able to afford to pay for the Salome Love Legacy, and even the possible loss of my promotion. Most of all, I cried for not being enough for the man I'd fallen for, Jonas Crane. Overwhelmed, I climbed off my bed and started running in place. Then I went down to the floor and did crunches. Sweat poured off my body as I ran and squatted on the floor, doing every exercise I could dream of. Pushing my body to the limit.

I'll make myself over. Like I did when Declan broke up with me. Somehow. My mouth was dry and my vision blurred until every piece of my body cried out in agony. But my thoughts racing through my head stopped. Crawling under the covers on my bed, I fell asleep.

Crushing pain. Physical and mental agony gripped me when my eyes opened. Or tried to as my eyelids were practically glued shut. Morbidly, I didn't want to wake-up, but it was too late.

The room was clothed in darkness, but I wasn't interested in time. I had plenty of time for reflection ahead of me. With no one in my life. Like it was two weeks ago. *Two weeks?* Impossible, but true. Jonas Crane filled every little piece of that time. Being in his presence, he seemed immense. Spending time with him seemed infinite. Nothing with him was inconsequential. I had fallen for him. His brand of attention, protection, and care.

Being his companion was by far the happiest time I had since my parents' death. I ended it because I became too attached, too soon. More of his company, and I'd never want to leave it. I wasn't good enough anyway. He pushed for me to expose my shame, my beaten face.

So I refused him. I covered my mouth as the realization hit me, just as severe as the blows I had sustained only the day before. I chose Declan. *Again.*

Perhaps Declan was right. We deserved each other. His hold was powerful, and I'd proven powerless. Forcing myself to my feet, I collected painkillers and headed to the kitchen to take them. The fragrance of the Tiger Lilies clogged my nostrils. Choking me on their sweet scent. I was a vagabond. *A liar. A weak, fat princess.*

The doorbell sounded.

"Lily, open up!" Natasha called out.

"Where is your key?" I called back. I frowned and stomped my bare feet over to the door, only to find it unlocked. "It's unlocked!" I jerked the door open wide.

Natasha strolled by me with shopping bags in her hands. "My hands were full." She strolled inside. "You shouldn't sleep all day."

I rolled my eyes and turned back to close the door.

"Lily," a voice called out. I turned and froze in place.

I inadvertently raised my hands, as if attempting to deflect an attack.

It was Dani Crane, Jonas's ex-wife, standing a few feet from me.

Dani's brows went north and her lips parted. "Lily…."

I burst into tears and fled from the door, reaching my bedroom door and moving to close it. I couldn't believe she was here, or my reaction. I could hear her behind me and didn't attempt to close my bedroom door. I was completely exposed. Not only as a liar, but also as someone who had allowed another person to hurt her. My throat ached, as if something was clawing it from the inside. Lying down on my bed, I curled on my side and closed my eyes. Weak and stupid.

I felt the bed dip next to me. A hand on my back. "No. Lily. You're not weak and stupid," Dani said, shaking her head. I didn't realize I must have muttered the words aloud. "You were hurt by someone. I want to know who and everything that happened. I'm calling Jonas—"

"Does he know you came here?" I asked.

"Yes. We were both concerned when you said you fell. And you told him you didn't want to see him anymore. Which, for the record, I don't agree with. But let's focus on what's at hand right now." The sound of a phone ringing alerted me to action. I didn't want Jonas to know about what had happened to me.

I held up my hands, gesturing wildly for her to stop.

"Please. Don't tell Jonas," I pleaded.

She frowned, but pressed end call. "Why not?"

I looked away. "It's not his concern. You know we're not … companions anymore."

"That wouldn't stop Jonas if you're hurt. He'd want to help," Dani said with conviction. But seeing the panic in my eyes, she paused. "Tell me everything that happened and let me help you. That's the only way I'll agree. But, Lily, I won't lie. I'll just ask Jonas to give you some time. You understand?"

She won't lie, like me. I nodded, swallowing hard as self-loathing settled in once again. "I don't want Jonas involved. It was a…." The word accident caught in my throat. I couldn't say it. Why? Looking into her soft brown eyes, I couldn't say the lie anymore. I looked down at my hands. They were trembling. "I want to put what happened behind me."

"I need to know more than that," Dani said as she reached out and stroked my hair.

"What are you even doing here? How did you get here…?" I said.

"I went with my instincts and called David to take me here after your text message," Dani said, rubbing my back.

"Why?" I asked. "You barely know me. Why do you want to help me?"

She smiled. "Because, what I know I like very much. You're sweet, smart, and kind. We Crane's don't walk away. You're stuck with us." She winked. "And I once volunteered at the Women's Shelter."

My bottom lip quivered as I said, "Thank you, Dani, but I'm not going to a shelter. I don't need help. I just want to put this behind me."

"No decisions at this moment. I'll get you some water, and we'll talk about it," Dani said, walking out of the room. I sat up in shock at her ease and marveled at her command. She and Jonas were so alike.

She returned with a glass of water and handed it to me. I drained it dutifully. She removed her Burberry jacket, came and sat down and rubbed my arm, waiting patiently for me to tell her what happened. "Lies only lead to more lies. Before you know it, you've lost yourself in lies." My father's words echoed through my mind and this time I didn't try to cover the truth and recalled how he used to finish that speech by saying, "You're better than that, Lily. You're a Salomé."

No more lying. I stared off and gave voice to as much that happened over lunch as much of it as I could find the words for. My need to have my actions understood littered my retelling. I did it for the photos and videos. It was sudden. Yes. I stayed through lunch because I wasn't ready to give up hope for them or Declan. When I was done, I felt empty.

"I take it this isn't the first time he did this to you?" Dani asked quietly.

I paused as I thought about her question. There had been a few other times, but they were so far in between that I didn't think of them as significant. I wasn't ever hurt severely. Did they count when it wasn't as severe? A shake, a shove? Do they count too? Was I making excuses? I didn't know. "A few in the past." I looked up at her, sure to find admonishment. She only gave back more empathy, her rubs on my arm comforting.

"He won't come around again. So it's over." I let the tears fall from my chin. "Declan assured me he was going to rehab," I continued, "So he's trying to get help."

"That's enough for now. But I will have more questions," Dani said. "I'll also need you to get some help."

My heart started to race. "I don't want to press charges. A man's life shouldn't be ruined for a moment's mistake."

She stared at me blankly, then exhaled long. "One thing at a time. I was thinking some more talking. But nothing at this minute. I want you to rest."

"You're leaving now," I said, my voice small. I sucked in air.

"Nope," Dani said. "I'm going to get you something to put on your sore face and some herbs to help you rest." She stood and made her way towards the door.

"Dani?" I called.

She turned back. "Yes, Lily?"

I dropped my head. "Thank you for listening and helping."

"I think you need a little more than the herbs," Dani said. She opened her arms and slowly closed them around me in a hug. I took it, wanting nothing more than to be held and comforted. I wanted my mom and dad, but they were gone. I wanted Jonas, but I pushed him away and may have very well lost him completely. I was alone, and I didn't want to be. Thankfully, Dani didn't question. Just held on to me.

Tiger Lily Part Two: Available Now

.

NOTES FROM AUTHOR

Domestic abuse and violence occurs within all ages, genders, ethnicities, backgrounds, and economic levels. It can be verbal, emotional, as well as physical. For information and support, please contact your local community services department or visit www.thehotline.org.

THANK YOU READERS!

If you enjoyed Tiger Lily Part One, please review. For information about the story and my author's blog, please visit my website:

www.ameliesduncan.com

I'd love to hear from you. You can reach me through my Facebook:

www.facebook.com/pages/Am%C3%A9lie-S-Duncan/572889196145981

or contact me through my website:

www.ameliesduncan.com

I'm also on Twitter:

twitter.com/AmelieSDuncan

SUBSCRIBE TO AMÉLIE S. DUNCAN'S MAILING LIST

To receive updates as well as a sneak peek at Chapter One, prizes, and updates on new releases, please sign up to be on her personal mailing list.

Subscribe now: http://eepurl.com/baQzb5

ACKNOWLEDGMENTS

Thank you to Alan, my husband, best friend and partner. Thank you for keeping me motivated. Thank you for understanding. I love you.

Thank you so much to the incredible group of people that helped me with Tiger Lily Part One. I truly appreciate it.

Thank you to Leah Campbell.

Thank you to Silvia Curry of Silvia's Reading Corner.

Thank you to Cassia Brightmore.

Thank you to Donna Rich.

Thank you to, Cassia, Hermione, and Deanna for beta reading.

Special Thanks to Rod, Gretchen, Robert for reading earlier drafts.

Thank you to Carol Eastman and Paul Salvette.

Thank you to all the bloggers and reviewers.

ALSO BY AMÉLIE S. DUNCAN

47422164R00165

Made in the USA
Middletown, DE
23 August 2017